THE MILITARY MUSTANG

The Journey From Enlisted to Officer

BRANDON W. SEYL

First edition

Hardcover ISBN: 979-8-9886293-1-3

Paperback ISBN: 979-8-9886293-3-7

Table of Contents

Foreword

From our first meeting, I knew there was something different, in fact special, about Brandon. He was the total package— superb technician, humble leader, and calming presence—in the midst of our stressful and demanding White House mission. I've watched, with great pride, as his journey continues! I hope you enjoy his thoughtful book as much as I did.

—Brigadier General (Ret) Chad D. Raduege, USAF

About this Book

The Military Mustang" is a captivating trio of short stories exploring three individuals' extraordinary journeys from enlisted servicemembers to commissioned officers.

Along the way, we share in the unique experiences of the exceptional individuals serving in both roles within the U.S. military.

In the annals of military history, the term "mustang" originated during the Civil War as a title bestowed upon officers who had transitioned from enlisted soldiers. While battlefield commissions are no longer common nowadays, all military branches still maintain programs allowing enlisted members to earn a cherished commission.

Drawing upon the symbolism of the mustang horse that is renowned for its tenacity and strength, the title of this book encapsulates these individuals' unmistakable essence of fortitude.

Like the wild mustang with its unyielding survival instincts, many enlisted soldiers come from disadvantaged backgrounds, having frequently faced poverty, broken families, limited opportunities, and a lack of mentorship.

However, it is all these personal trials that ultimately assist in shaping these personnel into the military's equivalent of the untamed mustang, cultivating a fierce and unwavering survival mentality that will serve them well in the field, propelling them toward their military goals.

Each unique tale in "The Military Mustang" revolves around the experience of a distinct character in a diverse historical period, each one embarking on his own profound journey of self-discovery.

As you navigate these pages, you too will encounter their valuable lessons, ones that will shape their identities, exemplifying the core qualities of a mustang officer. This book offers a fresh and powerful perspective on military careers, highlighting the steadfast resilience and staunch dedication required to serve in both enlisted and officer roles.

Whether you aspire to be a military officer or are simply curious, prepare yourself for an enlightening and captivating read in each short tale. "The Military Mustang" will leave you with a deeper understanding of the military experience and a newfound appreciation for those choosing to walk the path of a mustang officer.

Happy reading!

PART ONE:

THE BEAT OF A MUSTANG

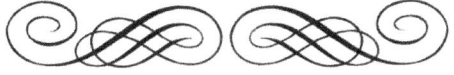

Lost in the Wild

Y our poor sons will have to pay with blood for the survival of the wealthy!"

The loud and haunting declaration pulsated through the otherwise still air, jolting Thomas from formerly placid thoughts. He had been languishing in his usual weathered chair at the wooden dining table, the sudden sound of a fracas nearby causing a swift glance across to Mother.

She was a woman of delicate stature with shoulder-length tresses of chocolate brown hair, whose visage, once a portrait of radiant grace, now bore signs of worry etched into fair but aged features. These days, Thomas barely recognized her as the vibrant woman she once had been. Now, her sunken eyes soon shifted toward the window of the cramped two-bedroom abode in which the family all somehow crammed themselves, her steps fueled by a mixture of dread and curiosity as she moved herself begrudgingly in the direction of the noises from outside, intent on peering out of the glass. She moved with such weariness, it seemed she barely had the strength to take these few steps. But she had to.

And it was something she had done many times before for similar reasons.

Like a woman furtively spying upon her next-door neighbor via the twitching of a voile curtain, she sought to investigate the latest commotion's source, letting nothing escape her knowledge. Her body shifted this way and that, twisting, gazing, and peering until finally, it seemed she had the fracas in sight. A huff of exasperated air escaped her lungs. Thomas sat quietly there, just waiting to see what she would say, if anything at all. The air was thick with tension.

He did not have to wait for long before she told her son what was going on.

Through the windowpane, his mother's had eyes met with a scene of disarray.

"They are flooding the town square," she said. "Oh, not again."

But of course, it was always going to be *again* and seemed it might never stop. Mother launched into a tirade, rambling on about the crowd's collective gestures. "They are frantic!" she complained. "And now, so am I!"

She described the people's unstoppable urgency, and as she spoke, the clamor of their voices merged with the rustling of newspapers, forming an unsettling cacophony of everyone's pent-up emotions, casting a surreal chaos over everything.

It was 1863 by now, and Father's death in the Battle of Manassas nearly two years earlier had delivered a grievous blow from which the family would never fully recover. Grief and anger, like relentless shadows, were still enshrouding the household even now, gripping their hearts with an unforgiving intensity, resolutely refusing to dissipate.

The news had arrived at this humble home in the form of a tattered letter from one of Father's fellow soldiers. A testament to the trials of war, the missive had borne witness to the sacrifices made on distant battlefields, and in its appearance, it too must have seen better times. The corner of the thin paper looked decidedly dog-eared, its once black ink blurred and faded to gray, the state of the writing presenting a challenge as the mother and two sons huddled close, grappling to comprehend its content.

Despite its shabby outer, there had still been no escaping the fact that it bore sorrowful tidings that seemed to seep from every smudged word.

Thomas was the younger of the two sons, no longer just a boy, but edging toward manhood. He still struggled to grow a moustache or beard and had barely begun shaving, but at times like this, the man in him was already surging to defend what little they possessed. The war having taken away the head of the household, it meant the two boys would need to step up. Especially, they needed to look after their mother, to keep her safe from harm.

Back to that dreaded letter from the front. If Thomas had not known better, he could have sworn someone's eyes had let droplets of their tears fall onto the paper before the letter even reached the family's hands, but it was all the doing of careless delivery, the letter having made its way to the small house by horse-drawn mail wagon, bearing a postage stamp of exactly five cents.

Though all the mail came by such a wagon, there had certainly been something strange that day, an unpleasant foreboding accompanying it. For one thing, they did not usually receive any letters except for those from Father, ones which had been all too irregular of late. No one had been expecting a letter on that day, anyway, and even when it had sat in Mother's shaking hands and she had read it aloud to her boys, for a few minutes, it was as if it still hadn't arrived.

No one would acknowledge it or shed a tear, the shock far too great for that. It was something they all had shrugged off, unable to believe it.

So, they'd sat and said, "Ah, well." Then Mother had risen and made pot after pot of hot black tea as if the magical potion could somehow bring her husband back. After that, she prepared to read the words aloud again, wide-eyed, while her beloved boys' own eyes began brimming with salty tears at last, reality finding a place in their psyches.

She clutched onto her elder son's hand while her trembling right hand held out the letter, even though she had finished the first read some time ago. "I may have misunderstood," she whispered. "Let us go through it a second time. What do you think, boys?"

She didn't wait for an answer. Her boys leaned close, their eyes connecting for a moment as if to say, *she's not willing to accept the truth of it.* In that brief exchange of glances, two young boys were forced into becoming men.

"Esteemed Mrs. Adam," the letter had begun, as Mother's hand trembled while she read, the words paying solemn tribute out of respect to the departed soldier.

"With great sadness, I impart the news of your beloved Charles' passing." And in that moment, the family's already small world had diminished even further, now standing still, the shadow of loss descending with merciless force as they stood there as if fixed to the spot, absorbing the reality of a future forever altered.

The letter went on to say, "He fought bravely in long, treacherous battles," a humble testimony indeed. Finally, it closed with, "I offer you my heartfelt condolences." It was all a feeble attempt to extend solace across an expanse of unfathomable loss and grief, reaching out with empathy and compassion. Yet there was also a businesslike air to it, one that gave away the fact that so many of these letters were being sent out daily. It was just "business as usual" to the sender.

Amidst the family's struggles of processing the news and the tapestry of war stories forever adorning the pages of the newspaper, a headline had also loomed large and ominous: *1861: Civil War Begins.* And in that moment, a personal journey of grief had intertwined with the unfolding tragedy now known to be engulfing the land.

The young men's mother, of course, had been bearing the brunt of it for two years now, something they could witness in her demeanor at all times, despite her saying barely anything at all. She often kept her lips pursed as if trying not to let questioning words escape against her will, her eyes brimming with tears she would not set free.

Her husband had died valiantly, and Thomas quietly believed she refused to show tears since that would be akin to acknowledging another defeat.

The boys both knew she was far too headstrong for that.

Her mind, too, had immediately become a battleground of her own, one in which anger and resentment waged relentless assault. Now, she would be carrying all the pain that had felled the whole family, a constant reminder of the wounds that even time could not heal.

Thomas remembered her shouting, directing a tempest of absolute fury at those "heartless bastards in office." Shaking the newspaper in her trembling hands, and with tears eventually cascading down her cheeks out of anger rather than self-pity or grief, she'd cried, "They haven't even been in power for a year! And now see what they've done!" Her voice had been a piercing lament. "They have already taken your father from us!"

***

Forced to pick up the pieces of their shattered lives in the two years that had since gone by, Thomas had soon found himself working three jobs to scrape by. Henry, the elder brother, possessed an irrepressible ambition, forever seeking opportunities promising him a chance of financial prosperity so that he could finally start his own business.

This drive motivated him to join the Union, a decision his mother bitterly opposed.

Now, don't get me wrong; Henry loved his mother and brother deeply but was desperate to escape. And who could blame him? Life had become an unending cycle of misery and struggles, the hideous memory of Father's death still clinging to the home and each of them like a shadow or persistent rain cloud, a grim reminder of a loss way too profound to shake off.

However, Henry's yearning for a brighter future clashed with the threesome's collective yearning to preserve this family's fragile vestige and unity.

As the war raged on, Thomas found himself growing more and more anxious by the day, caught up in an agitated state, unable to switch down a gear. The onslaught of war-related news was bombarding the boy's senses, overwhelming him with a pervasive helplessness and an unsettling uncertainty about the future. Amid all this chaos, he had to keep his family close and united.

Henry shot a worried look at their mother. "What's all this noise about?" he asked, his voice exhibiting concern.

Mother hesitated with her reply. "I'm not entirely sure," she said. "But it's got the whole city stirred up. Probably just some news from Washington about the war. No need to worry, boys. Same as usual. You know how it goes."

The *you know how it goes* was supposed to be some sort of a reassurance, but she would not have known it would have the opposite effect. Henry and Thomas looked at one another, their looks as if to say, *yes, we know how it goes. War, loss, misery, and yet more deprivation.*

But they knew better than not to worry, and they had known it for such a long time too.

In fact, even as she spoke the words "no need to worry," her face was loudly and bitterly lamenting a remarkably different tale, her expression one of defeat but also apprehension and fear. This was the demeanor of a woman who surely knew what was coming soon, what this family was in for. Her eyes looked afraid, no doubt just like the eyes of all the women who had in past generations seen husbands and sons depart for some other terrible front line, not always getting to see them come back.

Because of how anguished she looked, a growing unease had embedded itself in Thomas' gut, multiplying by the day—sometimes, by the hour if they heard of more agitation—a deep sense of foreboding that refused to be ignored. Whenever Mother attempted to dismiss such significant matters, it only fueled the boys' fears for the same reason I have mentioned already, that she was lousy at hiding any of the thoughts she was trying so hard to keep covert.

In time, Thomas noted how she began looking away when she answered their questions, undoubtedly aware that each time she attempted it, her boys would look at each other with glances of skepticism.

Besides, they were uneasy in their own rights, Thomas' exchange of concerned glances with Henry always revealing that he, too, had sensed this rapidly gathering storm. Something was brewing outside that would change their lives forever, and they both knew it. It was the same kind of certainty with which they would know whether it was sunny or rainy, summer or winter.

There was just no avoiding it.

Mother's repeated dismissal of what was happening around them could not make any difference for them whatsoever, and it was clear that she felt helpless to protect her boys. They crept around, afraid to upset her already volatile nerves that were forever on a knife edge, feeling so sorry for her, the woman who only wanted all her men at home and soon could end up with none.

If you had asked Thomas, however, he would have said that their mother always seemed more concerned about him than she was for Henry, the golden child of the two. At eighteen years old, Henry already possessed a magnetic charisma that made him a star at school, popular with his peers. His lofty ambitions seemed to set him apart, eager to carve out his own path in the vast expanse of the Western frontier; other boys flocked to him as something of a mentor, aspirational. No doubt their mother worried very little regarding Henry, she knew he would find a way one way or another.

Young Thomas, on the other hand, did concern her, and she showed it in her looks of worry and her frequent admonishments and advice to the boy.

Thomas was quieter and more introverted, content with staying close to home and helping the family make ends meet in more traditional, low-key ways.

Besides, as far as Thomas was concerned, he never really had the time or the opportunity to think about what he wanted to do. His mother wanted him to become a railroad worker like Father had been before he'd been pushed away to war. It seemed to be the natural thing for her younger boy as far as she was concerned.

But he had always seen the misery behind his father's eyes, knowing that he had forsaken his true passion for teaching, for the family.

He tried to hide it from Thomas and Henry, of course, but he had been no better at concealing bitter and uneasy truths than their mother was.

To Thomas' immense annoyance, though he loved Henry dearly, their mother also never stopped pushing him to be more like his brother, seeking to mold him into a reflection of Henry's achievements, urging him to "fulfill his untapped potential." Yet its true meaning was lost on Thomas. What did she mean by that? As far as he was concerned, his greatest potential and the thing he most craved to do was to be there with his family, to support them however he could, from the comfort and safety of his own home. He missed his father too, a man who had always cherished the simplest of joys as Thomas also felt he did. And now Father was gone, someone had to remain to be the man of the house, didn't they? *Bad things happen to women left alone when all the men went away, whether to war or to something else,* thought Thomas.

And even if nothing bad were to happen to their mother, there was no way he wanted to think she would be seen as a free woman by other men. Henry and he were not ready to see their father replaced, though they knew she was not looking to do so either. But if times were to grow hard in the young men's absence, a smooth-talking type could come along to weasel his way in, and young Thomas was having none of that. So, he would stay at home. That was settled, then.

At least, in his mind, it was.

His mother and brother always wanted more, however, but for now, they were all in one place. That was something for which Thomas was grateful. Together, day after day, they grappled with the relentless pursuit of sustenance, striving to put food on the table and keep the tiny roof over their struggling heads. But the war was already affecting everyone around, tearing families apart and leaving in its wake a trail of death and desolation. It was always there every second of the day, no matter what anyone was doing, an all-pervading oppressiveness from which none of them could escape, even if it hadn't directly come to their door except by stealing Father away.

The divide between the *haves* and the *have-nots* was becoming more starkly evident, painting a portrait of contrasting worlds. The privileged and the wealthy lived untouched by wartime's harsh realities. To them, the war had become an opportunity, a means to amass further riches. Meanwhile, the poor were left trembling under the weight of their fears, some even fleeing their homes out of desperation, in search of elusive sanctuary. The reality of war was stark and brutal, an undeniable truth etched upon the collective consciousness.

The screams and shouts outside only grew louder and more urgent, the boys' mother remaining paralyzed in the face of mounting chaos. Henry broke the uneasy silence, rising to his feet with a determined look. "All right, Thomas," he said. "Let's go see what's going on."

Grateful for his initiative and relieved that Henry had assumed the mantle of leadership, young Thomas trailed closely behind his elder brother as they made their way to the commotion outside.

His brother was the spitting image of their late father, tall and strong like Lincoln himself. His towering frame exuded strength, while his thick brown hair framed his face with piercing dark eyes that held power to set hearts aflutter. He even had a bit of stubble, something Thomas envied in his permanently futile efforts to grow something resembling a beard.

On the other hand, no one would deny Thomas resembled their mother, a fact that Henry, in his playful jests, would never allow him to forget. He would taunt his brother with good-natured banter about their "vast" height difference, for Thomas stood a few inches shorter than his towering figure. But their mother always defended her younger son by reminding him that he was still growing into a man, and besides, there was nothing wrong with lacking height.

The height of a man, she insisted, did not determine status or success; it was all a myth, she postulated, coming to short Thomas' defense like a mama bear to her cubs'.

However, in spite of all this, while he lacked the physical attributes of maturity, he was still aspiring to one day match both his brother's physical stature and presence.

Stepping out into the scorching heat, Thomas followed Henry's footsteps, his eyes squinting against the blinding brilliance of the sun. Yet the throngs of people in the streets quickly overshadowed everything else. In the bustling city of Harrisburg, everyone had grown accustomed to witnessing crowds, but this was different.

A palpable tension existed between them, fueling a sense of urgency that caused the tiny hairs on the back of the neck to stand on end.

The boys' parents always insisted that living here would create opportunities for them, but as they looked around at the anxious sea of faces, Thomas began to doubt what he viewed as dubious promises. Living in the city only invited heartache, thrusting them into all this madness. A sliver of longing crept within his mind that a life full of riches could perhaps have offered a different, more sheltered experience.

As the two boys pushed through the crowd, Thomas felt Henry's hand come to rest upon his shoulder. "Don't wander off, all right? We stay together," he mandated. Thomas nodded solemnly.

They soon were standing in front of the city chapel, a group of fervent women seeking solace there in prayers resonating with a haunting fervor. The sound filled Thomas with unease, and he couldn't help but wonder if they had already lost the war. As he eavesdropped on the conversation, the tension heightened. An elderly couple a few steps away evidently found themselves on the precipice of despair, gasping. They yelled, "But if we give more, we won't be able to care for the city. This is an outrage! They cannot do this to us!"

Caught off guard, Henry and Thomas found themselves jolted by a force that abruptly pressed upon their bodies, knocking the wind out of their chests. In a flash, both boys spun around, ready to defend themselves against an unseen enemy.

But their defenses lowered; it was only Henry's best friend, Samuel, saying hello in his usually effusive way.

Although they all went to the same school, Thomas couldn't say he particularly liked the guy. He was a year older than the two of them, shorter than Henry—closer to his own height—and with a round, pale face and hopeful eyes. His features lent him an air of youthfulness and innocence. He had more hair on his face than on his head, but always dressed to impress, with a well-tailored, long-sleeved cotton shirt and a pair of immaculate black trousers.

But what truly set Samuel apart was his family's wealth. His parents were known to own the Harrisburg Railroad, a business transporting thousands of Union troops and supplies. While the rest of society was struggling to make ends meet, Samuel's family thrived through the spoils of war. Despite their kindness toward Thomas and Henry's family, Thomas could not help but hold resentment against him, a barrier erected by the disparities existing between the two households.

"What's all the rumpus, Sam?" Henry asked urgently as Samuel greeted them with a look of exuberance and excitement.

"President Lincoln has signed the Conscription Act, effective immediately," he revealed, his tone bearing a tinge of expectation.

"What does that mean exactly?" Thomas asked, a sinking feeling settling in his stomach, dreading the onslaught of more terrible news.

Samuel explained, "There aren't enough men to fight the war, so President Lincoln's ordered military drafts for all men between the ages of eighteen and thirty-five."

Oh no. Thomas' spirits dived at the thought of the devastation it would inflict upon their poor mother. He turned to gaze at Henry, seeing a broad smile spreading across his face, as radiant as the summer sun.

"That's great news!" Henry exclaimed as if someone had bestowed him a tremendous fortune. "Once the greybacks are dealt with, I'll finally be able to travel West!"

Samuel chuckled, saying, "Boy, you're crazy for wanting to fight, especially after everything that's happened."

But Henry was undeterred, puffing his chest out proudly, his chin high. "Look, I don't care about the reason for the war anymore," he declared. "It's personal, yes. But this is a gateway to the life I've been yearning for. Like I said, I can finally start my life out West!"

As Henry leaned in, Samuel whipped out a newspaper that had been tucked discreetly within his back pocket. Thomas could already smell the terrible news coming, just in the way he produced it with such a flourish. "The names have already been selected. Notifications will be going out in two days," Samuel whispered, his words carrying an air of secrecy.

Samuel looked around, surreptitious as if seeking to avoid anyone overhearing despite the fact it was public news already and was all over the town by now.

Henry's bushy eyebrows shot up to his hairline as he implored, "Do you know if I'm on the list?" He tried to peer over his friend's shoulder. Samuel released the paper to him.

"You take a look," he said, and Henry did. Or he was about to, anyway.

Driven by anxiety, Thomas, his face pinked, grabbed the newspaper from his brother, his eyes silently pleading with him. "Please don't show this to Mother," he then said. "She's not coping well. I'm worried about her. The last thing she needs is to think she'll lose you—maybe both of us—to the war. Don't you think she's lost enough with our father's death?"

Henry looked at Thomas with a serious expression. "Now, listen here. She will be okay, Thomas," he reassured, though Thomas had no idea what he was basing his assertions upon. "I will ensure that she's taken care of." Despite his intentions, however, his words only served to remind the younger brother of all their father's empty promises before he had deserted them. How could they not remind him of that? They were two of a kind, Henry and the boys' father.

Overwhelmed, Thomas lashed out at his brother. "Yes, well, don't forget our father once spoke of similar things," he spat out bitterly. But as the words escaped his lips, he instantly regretted them. This was his dear brother, the one he loved and looked up to; it never came easily to create any kind of a rift between them. But his frustration and anxiety were mounting. He wanted Henry to stay, craving the stability they'd had before everything had begun to disintegrate.

But little did he know that in two days' time, their mother would sink deeper into depression, unraveling the fragile threads fastening them all together.

For one thing, if Henry took himself off to war, where would the finances come from to feed the family and to keep their mother away from the debt collectors? Thomas could not do it all alone. The thought of working three jobs to support the family filled him with dread, and he also wondered, was he even desperate enough to consider working for Samuel's parents?

The thought itself disgusted him, making him nauseous.

Thankfully, Thomas' brother chose not to acknowledge the hurtful remarks; he would not retaliate, perhaps driven by the same thoughts that had pervaded Thomas' mind, that they were kin and war was never worth two brothers fighting over. Especially not boys who had grown as close as anyone could be. He was like the other half of Thomas.

Instead of putting up an argument, Henry offered only a soft-spoken voice and words of comfort, though they did little to assuage Thomas' concerns. "You will be okay," he reassured yet again, his voice bearing a hint of stubborn determination. "Our commitment to our family is what truly matters." His words almost brought a smile to Thomas' lips, but the reality of the situation quickly brought him back to earth.

Yes, Henry, he thought. *Our family. The one you are abandoning by hoping to see your name on the list of conscripts. How does your disappearance help Mother and me?*

He didn't dare speak the words aloud, only imploring Henry further with his gaze. It did not achieve a thing. As he held onto the newspaper, everything felt as if it settled on his chest. Compressing his lungs, asphyxiating him. It was time to confront his fears and find a way to move forward, no matter how difficult.

Henry and Thomas pushed through the swelling crowd, saying their goodbyes to Samuel and wishing him luck. Then, they meandered homeward side by side, silent as they each mused on their separate thoughts. In any other circumstance, one of them would have asked the other what he was thinking, but just now, there was no point in it—and they also did not dare.

Stepping over the threshold of their tall, blue door, they were met with the same sight they had left behind, their mother perched on the couch, her eyes brimming with annoyance.

They exchanged a worried glance, bracing themselves for the impact of their impending announcement. And in this moment, they were again united, Thomas and his brother, united against the anger to come their way. He waited for Mother to speak. She did not, only pursing her lips all the more, gazing in the direction of her boys while scarcely daring to meet their eyes.

It was the prompt for which Henry would have been waiting. If she did not know about the conscription, she would have quizzed them both about where they had been and what they'd been doing, but it was clear some dreadful thought or other was holding her back.

What else could it be?

"You have probably heard there aren't enough men, Mother," Henry began after clearing his throat, his words cowed with tension. "They're drafting all able-bodied men in two days' time."

She looked momentarily straight at him, then her dark eyes flashed away again as if she couldn't bear to look at her usually precious boy right now. The atmosphere grew dense, suffocating. The scorching sun seemed to follow them all inside, sweat no doubt trickling down their backs.

Mother stood up dramatically, her eyes blazing with fury. "Of course, they are. They want to sacrifice our sons!" she exclaimed.

Her words, though spoken softly, resonated with an undeniable conviction. "And for what? So that we can dictate who can enslave others or not?"

With a swift stride, she stormed off to her bedroom, slamming the door behind her. And that was that. Henry and Thomas were alone once again.

For a moment, the room filled with palpable tension. But then, unexpectedly, the boys breathed a collective breath of relief. Surprisingly, their mother's response had oddly been better than they had expected. It was briefer, anyway, and that would do for now.

On the fateful day of the draftee announcement, Thomas and his family joined the town's gathering area, their hearts weighted with fear and unease. Anticipation reigned, the crowd eerily quiet and the only sound was the relentlessly impatient *tap-tapping* of the announcers on the stage several feet away.

Standing in close proximity to Samuel's family, young Thomas couldn't help but notice their composed and calm demeanor, contrasting with his tense and anxious state. They gave sympathetic nods, their faces a mask of concern. But a trace of smugness seemed to be lurking there beneath the surface, as if they knew something they felt certain the other families didn't.

As the moment of truth approached, a knot formed in Thomas' stomach.

Who among them would they choose? Would it be someone he loved? Fear and dread consumed him, setting his pulse quickening. Finally, the announcement began, the tension nearly unbearable. The announcer's voice boomed across the gathering area, commanding everyone's focus. "Attention, attention! By the Conscription Act of 1863, signed by President Lincoln, all male citizens between the ages of eighteen and thirty-five are subject to a military draft."

With each passing moment, Thomas' nerves were on edge, his heart pounding in his chest. Then came the pivotal moment: "The following men have been selected for service through a randomized draft lottery selection process."

Before the boys could react, their mother unleashed an anguished scream, her voice piercing through the crowd. "Great God! What has this country come to?" she yelled, her fury pouring out unchecked. Everyone turned with expressions of empathy and sorrow, and the family huddled together, the boys holding their mother close.

For a moment, the announcer's gaze met Mother's own with deep sadness before regaining his composure, continuing with the draftee announcement. Despite the noise and chaos around, life as they had known it would never be the same again.

"William Gates.

"Samuel Gaty.

"Theodore Aackley.

"Charles Bevens.

"Henry Adams."

As the announcer continued to list names, Thomas' mother shrieked out the kind of agonizing wail of a tormented animal before she crumpled to her knees, her body wracked with uncontrollable sobs. Henry and Thomas exchanged a look of deep concern before scooping her up and hurrying home. As for Thomas, he was torn in two, his heart cleaved; Henry would be going away to fight, and he would stay home with Mama. It was just as he had been wishing for himself, so why did it make him feel so abysmally wretched? Perhaps the separation from Henry would be too much. What if he just never came home again like Father?

Thomas stood by and watched as his mother and Henry embraced each other tightly, seeing simultaneously the grin on his face and the relief in his eyes, knowing that he would fight for the Union, something of which he had been dreaming for quite some time now. But it was all set against the backdrop of pent-up tension in the room as their mother's heart fragmented into a million pieces, knowing she would be losing another dear person to this heinous war.

Henry gripped their mother tightly, whispering soothing words into her ear. "It's all right, Ma. I will be back before you know it. I want to do this. I want to fight for our country. This is what I need to do. And of course, I am doing it for Father too. You want this wrong to be corrected, don't you?"

How could she possibly put up a resistance against that kind of argument? It seemed so unfair of Henry to voice it thus. But to Thomas' astonishment, she did fight back.

Tears streamed down Mother's face as she looked up at him, a good foot in height between them. "And what good would that do, Henry?" she cried out, her voice choked with pain. "How many young boys need to die for this war to end? What good is it if I keep losing my loved ones to this senseless war? So, you will rectify one loss by delivering to me a second one?"

Her words turned into a whisper edged with pain. "I can't bear the thought of losing you too, Henry. You boys are all I have left. After your father's passing, I promised myself I wouldn't lose anyone else, and here we are, and you are telling me you'll be enlisting. How do you think that makes me feel? Well, I'll tell you! My heart can't take it anymore. Please..."

Henry stood up, straightening himself, staring at his mother with a fiery passion in his eyes. "I promise you Ma, I will come back with greater hope for our future. You need to believe in me." The room fell silent as Thomas' mother leaned onto the wall as if it was all she had left.

Now, it was Thomas' turn to cling to Henry, his arms wrapping tightly around him, desperately trying to imprint the sense of his brother's presence upon his memory. The specter of uncertainty bore down upon them, and tears welled up in Thomas' eyes too. As Henry held onto him, reluctant to let go, he whispered, "Take care of Ma, and stay strong." His voice quivered. "Remember that family is everywhere, even in the most unexpected places. And if the worst should come to pass…" His voice threatened to crack. "If it should, then you will both be all right. In time, you will be…"

Thomas nodded, his throat constricted with unspoken words, unable to find any voice in that moment of farewell. How could it be just and deserved that he would leave immediately? How would a few more days of their family's togetherness make a difference to a war that had been so long in the making? But Thomas understood that it did, and Henry would need to go soon.

Henry's gaze met his brother's, a mixture of love and concern shining through his tears. "Promise me you'll look after her," he implored. "She needs you now more than ever."

With a sorrowful heart, Thomas nodded again as more tears made their way down his cheeks.

The next few hours were a blur as they moved, gathering Henry's belongings and packing them with care. Each item they carefully folded and placed into the bags was another stark and cruel reminder of Henry's impending departure. Between the flurries of activity, their mother's anguish was palpable. She slowly grabbed onto Henry's shirt, tugging at the fabric, voice choked with sorrow. "Why must it be this way?" she cried out. "My boy, my boy!"

Henry knelt before her, holding onto her trembling hands as he declared, "I promise you, Ma, I will return to you, and I'll come back home stronger than ever. And when I do, I will lift you high upon my shoulders. Like this…"

And with that, he stood up to embrace her one last time, lifting her from her feet, swinging her high. She looked so diminutive against his frame. He was already a soldier, and she was already a mother who had no say in anything. She tried to laugh, crying out, "Put me down, ye great lump!"

But that only made him worse, and in the end, she cried harder at the joy of it before he set her down again on the ground. They stood, foreheads together, before he kissed her cheek and wiped her tears away with each hand. "Shh, Ma. I will be home before you know it."

After Henry's efforts to comfort their mother, they stepped out of the home, shoulders and moods struggling under the oppressiveness of the moment as if a great shroud had fallen upon them all. The familiar streets leading them to the train station seemed to echo with unspoken fears, silent yet pregnant with noise.

At the station, the three stood as a family, united by heartache as Henry boarded the train with the other young recruits. Thomas watched as Henry turned to him and to their mother, his face a mixture of steadfast focus and incongruous vulnerability.

"Take care of yourselves," he called out, his voice carrying a blend of love and longing. "I will carry you both in my heart until we meet again."

Then Thomas' lips started to mirror the bitter smile that Henry carried. Mother's lips twisted into a strained curve upwards. God only knew how everyone still found a way to try and look happy.

The train slowly pulled away, its wheels grinding against the tracks, Henry standing by the window to wave goodbye until he could not be seen at all anymore, his two family members just holding onto the sound of the trundling metal wheels as the train picked up speed.

A lump formed in Thomas' throat as terrible thoughts filled his head. *What will become of him? What if he never returns to us?* The four-part rhythm of the train's motion in the distance formed a sorrowful tune with which Thomas' thoughts sought to fit, a stanza of *what if he dies, what if he dies, what if he dies...?*

And with that, Henry was gone, and Thomas wanted to give out that same visceral howl his mother had let free earlier in the day. He did not let it loose, swallowing his misery instead.

Thomas dared not speak those thoughts aloud as beside him, his mother stood quietly, her face an emotionless mask. Her eyes betrayed the depths of her turmoil, but she remained stoic as if she wasn't there, almost as if her body stood there on the platform alongside Thomas, while her spirit had departed with their beloved Henry.

Thomas glanced sideways, then held her tightly, the only comfort he could offer in that moment. If indeed it felt like anything at all. Samuel, who had stood by them both, tried to make a joke to lighten the mood and distract them from the uneasiness. But it was difficult to find humor in a situation so grave. His efforts were misplaced, especially as Samuel had managed to secure his own exemption through a hefty payment of three hundred dollars, a fortune this family could only dream of earning in a year. As the two stood there with their wealthy friend accompanying them, they couldn't help but feel the injustice of the situation weighing heavily upon them.

Anyway, Thomas told himself, *Henry wanted to go. He was excited about it. So even if Samuel had offered to lend us the money, Henry would never have accepted the offer to extricate him.*

The Conscription Act had its exemptions, favoring the wealthy and influential. It left the less fortunate with little choice but to serve in the army, this factor in itself leading to weeks of violent riots and unrest. Uneasiness settled in upon Thomas and his mother now, casting a shadow of uncertainty over their future. Now, he was responsible for taking care of their mother—and she was responsible for taking care of him. They had only each other.

***

The following months passed in a blur of exhaustion and despair. With Henry gone and their mother's health rapidly deteriorating, a burdensome sense of responsibility pressed heavily upon Thomas' young shoulders. Soon enough, he was juggling three jobs that were barely enough to put food on the table for even the two of them. Times were growing harder now, a bleak depression setting in, and even the staple goods were commanding unreachable prices in the town's stores. Thus, each day became a relentless cycle of labor, leaving him physically and emotionally drained, but he was desperate. No, *they* were desperate. Had he existed alone, it would have been easier for he could have made do with less.

But one look at Mother, and he worked harder, longer, owing it to Henry and to Pa.

In the mornings, he would wake before dawn, stumbling out of bed with half-closed eyelids and aching muscles. The bitter chill of the early morning air accompanied Thomas to his first job at the local bakery. The scent of freshly baked bread greeted him there, a faint glimmer of comfort amidst the weariness. Mixing dough, kneading it with cracked hands, he would watch the hours blur together, lost in the repetitive motions. They would slip away, time blending into a constant cycle of mixing, baking, and serving.

After cleaning up at the bakery, he would rush to a storage facility nearby, finding himself in warehouses, loading and unloading crates, the sweat trickling down both brows and forehead as he strained against the weight of the world. The labor would take a toll on his body, leaving him exhausted and sore, but he would push through regardless, knowing he had no other choice.

And then, before the sun could finally set, he would be at the factory, the noise and clamor of machinery drowning his thoughts and himself in a sea of monotony. He would be running around, assigned to various tasks, assembling parts or tending to the production line. The repetitive motion became a relentless dance, blurring the line between day and night. A cog in a vast machine, he was constantly working, persistently stuck.

In between physical exhaustion and the constant juggling of jobs night and day, he was confronted with the overwhelming challenge of his own inexperience. Guilt became a constant companion, whispering into his ears, *Am I doing enough? Could I have done more?*

All this was threatening to crush Thomas, losing him in a world he wasn't prepared to navigate.

And then, as if fate could not spare them, his worst fears came true. Mother's condition had worsened. The doctors were calling it a fever, but to Thomas' mind, it could be nothing other than a symptom of her shattered heart. The bitterness, desperation, and anger had consumed her. He held her frail hands in his own, wishing that somehow, she could escape the unbearable pain. But in the face of such overwhelming grief, helplessness overcame him, leading the boy to drown in a sea of sentiments over which he had no control.

Days turned into nights, and nights into days, as he watched her strength ebb away, standing by helpless, nothing to do but to beg once more for help from the doctors who in turn declared they could do nothing at all. So, he would stand by again, wringing his hands.

Guilt was bearing down on Thomas, threatening to break him.

Now, he was questioning every decision that he had made, every sacrifice endured, wondering if it had all just been in vain. Soon, it appeared that it had been. All the effort, the tears, the anguish, and the pleading had been for nothing, and as his mother's breaths grew shallow and her grasp on life slipped away, he clung onto her with all his might, whispering words of love and hoping that somehow, she could hear him. Among his words, he said goodbye to her from Henry too.

By now, he hoped she would not know which son he was, only that it was one of them, if she even heard Thomas' voice at all. "We won the war, Mama, and I came back to you," he lied.

In the end, as he stood by her bedside, her body still and her eyes closed, he couldn't help but feel his immense vulnerability, uncertainty, and doubt overwhelming him. Thomas had become small again like a child, a lost waif wandering parentless, no siblings either, cast into solitude.

As the shadows of the evening drew long and began to bring a foreboding and lonely darkness to the house, she heaved a final breath, opening wide her eyes and staring at her son a final time. Her arm raised for the briefest of moments as if seeking to pluck a feather from thin air before it dropped like a stone. Perhaps it was Father she reached for. Then she was gone.

Thomas sat there staring at her lifeless body, immobile, loneliness and heartbreak pressing in on him like a ton of bricks. His family, the pillar of his existence, had been torn away. With both parents now gone and Henry at war, the house felt empty and desolate. No more family dinners, no more shared moments of joy, only the hollow echo of a life that had been shattered. The house felt alien now, just bare stone and mortar, cold walls, an echoing tiled floor that seemed to laugh back at the footsteps that, these days, were only ever Thomas' own.

That house was ridiculing him now, taunting, *now what will you do?*

Days turned into weeks, and the funeral came and went.

The presence of well-wishers and neighbors only ever accentuated the emptiness consuming the boy. Even Samuel's generous offer of a job at the train station, promising stability, felt hollow. Besides, why would a man ever want to choose a job at a train station when he had waved away—and cried away—his only brother from that hideous place?

Was Samuel's suggestion some kind of sick joke? No, it was not. But even so, it knifed Thomas in the heart each time he even allowed himself to think of it. The thought of a life devoid of purpose, akin to his father's, sickened him now more and more. How could he bear the thought of slogging through each day without his family? What would be the purpose in that?

The image of his mother's lifeless body haunted him too, leaving a void in Thomas' heart that could never be filled. No job, no orphanage, not even the idea of joining the war itself could replace the love and bond shared with a family. The other men's sacrifices for their country weighed on him, making the notion of fading into obscurity an unbearable betrayal of their memory. It became painfully clear that nothing could replace the love and stability he had lost.

"Time heals," people would say. Well, they were either fools or liars; he could never work out which. It was just a platitude, a banal saying by those who had no idea of how it was to lose everyone. He could gladly have told them how it really was if only they had asked; he would have said it had left him adrift, lost in a world that felt foreign and cold, tears streaming down his face almost daily as he gazed out of the window, watching fat raindrops sliding down the glass.

He would have said how cold it felt nowadays in that godforsaken house in which he never even bothered to build a fire anymore because the place itself had no soul. There was no sense in trying to be artificially warm; the warmth he needed came from connections, ones that had been torn away. Now, he was left with such limited options, and they all felt wrong. He could work nonstop, join an orphanage, or even fight in the war like his brother and late father had done.

But none of it could begin to heal the void inside of him.

The war had taken everything, the happy life he'd once known, the people he'd held dear, and even his own sense of identity. He was a broken shell, left to pick up the shattered pieces of a life that could never be made whole again.

Lost and Found

And so it was that against all better judgment, he came to be standing yet again on a train station platform. The relentless midday sun was bearing down, its scorching rays searing the side of Thomas' face while a crisp and devious breeze breathed life into his otherwise weary soul.

The rhythmic thunder of the approaching train reverberated through the platform like a heartbeat pulsating with anticipation. Its steady cadence filled the surrounding space, occasionally interrupted by the screech of metal upon metal, bringing with it the odor of molten iron. The sour smell of travelers soon began wafting Thomas' way, a heady cocktail of long unwashed humanity mingling with the acrid smell of the train's brakes and its burning fuel.

With his gaze fixed upon the worn pages cradled within his hands, the name *Philadelphia* stared back at Thomas, inked in bold letters. And amidst the distractions, he couldn't help but wonder, lost in his own reverie, *is it even possible to run away from home if I'm the only one left behind?*

Guilt gnawed at the boy, a terrible burden upon his heart as he contemplated the memories he was leaving behind in Harrisburg. The thought of abandoning the family's precious belongings, the remnants of a life he had known and relished, filled Thomas with great sadness even despite that wretched house making him feel like a stranger there these days. It was still the only place that held onto memories once loved, ones still treasured forever.

But was this nothing but a fool's errand? Would distance truly have the power to fade the painful memories that haunted him, or would he, inside a month, a year, or a few years, find himself back where he'd started, alone again in those four barren walls, looking for his next escape?

In fact, maybe he would return and find the house gone; anything could happen to it in the time he was away. Deep down, there was an awareness that nothing would turn out simple from now on.

The only person who knew of Thomas' impending departure was Samuel since he had bought him his one-way ticket to a new life. Thomas had to admit, Samuel was pleasant enough and certainly had his moments of such generosity, but Thomas had still refused to work for him.

It had felt like a split-second decision, but at last, Thomas' heart and head were in unison. He was heading to Philadelphia to join the Union Army Infantry, to march alongside those brave souls united in the pursuit of a cause greater than themselves. He'd even entertained the idea of finding his brother and fighting alongside him in his unit, but alas, that was not going to be.

Thomas had discovered he was still too young.

Patriotic fever had motivated countless men, nearly 100,000 of them, no less, to enlist in the Union Army. Thomas had heard stories from his father, tales of young boys who, despite their tender years, had donned the uniform in defense of their country. Yet Thomas' own resolve to join the ranks was not rooted in patriotism, and if it had been, he would have enlisted sooner.

No, this was a deeply personal quest fueled by the desire to carve out a future that the war could not strip away, a chance at family and happiness in a time of post-war peace.

As Thomas' train drew nearer, he clutched onto thoughts of Philadelphia as if it were a lifeline to the new existence for which he yearned. With each passing moment, the rumble of the approaching train grew louder, echoing through the station, vibrating through his being and bringing with it the many memories he tried to swallow down along with the lump forming in his throat. They were the recollections of him and his mother standing here seeing Henry off, watching his train becoming a minuscule gray dot disappearing beneath a bridge.

He shed more tears for the fact that his mother never did see her elder boy again, and that many a time, Thomas had lied to her himself, being the one to tell her she would. But even if he had known better, he still would have been bound by honor to tell her the same.

And then, breaking into melancholy, the moment of departure arrived, swift and decisive.

Boarding the train, he found himself a seat, settling into the worn cushion as the wheels screeched in protest again, still hot from braking, the train lurching forward. The journey had begun, and his thoughts raced, a whirlwind of hopes and dreams intertwining with the rhythmic trundling of the wheels upon the track. Harrisburg slipped away; a fading memory left in the distance as the train hurtled toward its ultimate destination.

Inside the carriage, the atmosphere was a microcosm of society itself. From the worn-out travelers to starry-eyed dreamers, each individual carried worn hopes, aspirations and burdens.

Seated across from Thomas, an elderly couple sat in quiet companionship, their hands clasped together, a testament to a lifetime of shared experiences. The lines etched on their weathered faces spoke of a journey filled with both joy and sorrow. This was a love that had stood the test of time, a flame that continued to flicker even in the twilight of their years.

Farther down the aisle, a group of young soldiers exuded a contagious sense of camaraderie. Clad in crisp starched uniforms, their eyes gleamed with exuberance and intent, animated conversations rising to a crescendo as they exchanged tales of training, aspirations and boundless courage that united them. Their youth belied the burden of the responsibilities they willingly shouldered. And, of course, Thomas saw the irony in that.

Families huddled together, their children's laughter ringing out like chimes of hope amidst the clattering of wheels. Businessmen in sharp suits and hats exuded an air of purpose, their eyes focused on distant horizons. A group of artists, sketchbooks in hand, absorbed the passing landscapes, their eyes capturing the beauty that surrounded them in strokes of creativity.

And then there were those who appeared lost in their own worlds, solitary figures gazing out of the windows, their eyes filled with a blend of nostalgia and longing as if the passing scenery stirred dormant memories within. A young woman clutched a worn photograph, her fingers tracing the faded image with both fondness and sadness, lost in her daydream that transcended the confines of the train.

Conversations drifted in and out of earshot, melodies in an ever-changing symphony, occasionally metamorphosing into a sound like the buzzing of thousands of wasps or the giggling of children in a playground, in and out, fading and surging. The cadence of languages and dialects intermingled too, each carrying its own unique rhythm and inflection. Snippets of laughter, murmurs of concern, and whispers of shared secrets. In that confined space, they each embarked on this collective journey, forever connected by the irrevocable passage of time.

As Thomas held a tight grip on his ticket, the train's brakes screeched to a halt, jolting his heart with anticipation. He leaned forward, his eyes drawn to the large wooden sign that proudly read, *Welcome to Philadelphia.* As he peered outside, a bustling scene came into view, brimming with eager faces radiating hope and excitement. Faces pressed close to the window, hands cupping around eyes, attempting to see who was inside. They had come to meet someone off the train.

Of course, there was no one there to meet Thomas. It brought the familiar pang of loss to his gut.

Amidst the flurry of disembarking passengers, a sight caught him by surprise: Union soldiers stepping onto the platform. He couldn't help but feel a wave of curiosity about these men who had dedicated their lives to fighting for what they believed in. And here he stood too, off to fight. But what did he believe in and subscribe to, other than family, love, and companionship? None of those was a good reason to want to join the Union, yet here he was, feeling like a fool.

But there was no time for that, no time to chastise himself.

Curiosity piqued, Thomas scanned around to see who else was getting off the train, hoping to spot someone who would share his enthusiasm for the Philadelphia adventure ahead. It was fair to say the train had been filled with a mix of people from all walks of life, each with their reason for embarking on this journey. The atmosphere still buzzed with anticipation, a chorus of conversations and the shuffling of feet intermingling into a heady hum.

Thomas' focus remained steadfast on the horizon of possibilities, telling himself there was no greater thrill than a new future full of opportunities. His heart was set on exploring every inch of this vibrant and bustling city, determined to make it happen no matter what lay ahead.

As he stepped off the train, the energy of the city coursed through his veins, igniting a fire within. The adventure had only just begun, and he was ready to embrace it with open arms.

Then his heartbeat quickened. A man adorned with three blue stripes on his uniform commanded attention. His authoritative voice echoed across the platform, resounding with purpose. "Attention, all members of the 70th Infantry regiment, present yourselves over yonder!"

In an instant, the area filled with about 150 men, surrounding the one with stripes as he barked orders and conducted roll calls.

Thomas watched in awe as the man hollered out a flurry of names with firm authority, each soldier responding with conviction, proclaiming, "present and accounted for", or a loud grunt to acknowledge.

It became immediately evident that these men were recruits from the Camp Union, united in their commitment to serve. They appeared older than him, yet he had already resolved to tag along. It had been in his mind ever since packing to leave home, and now, ensnared in the crowd's encouragement of these brave men, it was the only thing to do. Of course, joining by adding himself to an established band of recruits haphazardly encountered was not the conventional way, but the opportunity had presented itself.

The onlookers couldn't help but pause in admiration and gratitude, their hearts filled with appreciation for the sacrifice and dedication of these brave soldiers. Prayers and well wishes permeated everything and everyone, the crowd extending them as a collective hope for the fighting men's safety and success.

As the man in stripes finished the roll call, he looked at the sea of faces before him and announced, "Hail and well met, brave and gallant soldiers! I bid ye a hearty welcome to the 70th Infantry Regiment. Our current mission is to march toward Gettysburg with all due haste. We have a two-day journey yonder till we rendezvous with our commanding officer, hence 'tis imperative that we tread with swift steps and vigor." He paused, scanning the crowd before saying, "Grab your belongings and let's move out."

Without hesitation, the men followed behind him, each with a fierce resolve etched on their faces. They were heading out on a new adventure that could hold the key to their future and the fate of this country. As Thomas watched them, something inside him stirred again, and before he knew it, he too was following the men, even more caught up in their energy and excitement.

It was an interesting decision, one he believed he had made much earlier, but now, seeing the men, something in his heart told him he had been correct. He had to be a part of this, no matter the cost. That's if they would have him, anyway! Suddenly, it struck him:

What if they turn me away?

Trailing behind like a lost pup, trying to keep up but also seeking to stay out of sight, he had never felt so out of place while at the same time so thoroughly wishing to be a part of something.

The scorching sun still beat down, intensifying the fatigue that settled upon Thomas' weary frame. His steps became sluggish, and each stride soon felt like a monumental effort. Sweat went trickling down his brow, mingling with the grime that clung to his skin while an acidic hunger gnawed at his stomach as if both intestines and guts were devouring themselves. It was all a reminder of the hours that had passed without respite. He couldn't help but mutter to himself in a desperate plea for relief, "When will we rest?"

A few men up ahead were turning around time and again; they had eventually noticed Thomas following them and begun whispering to each other, casting wary glances in the straggler's direction. But it was one of the men, a skinny but short fellow with sad eyes, who finally slowed his pace and turned to confront him. He grabbed at Thomas' arm.

Thomas saw how the man's forearm and wrist were even thinner compared to his own, something he'd never really seen before. There was more meat on a matchstick.

"What reasons have ye, lad, for tailing us?" the man asked, his tone cautious yet inquisitive. He lowered his head in the manner of a schoolmistress peering through her glasses.

Thomas could tell that the man was about the same age as his brother, Henry, but much leaner and paler. He eyed him with a mixture of exhaustion and uncertainty. "I ran away from home, and I'm not entirely sure where I'm going," he admitted. "I'd be grateful for any advice."

The man's expression softened, and he glanced briefly at his comrades. "The lad's lost," he called out. "Needs help to find where he's headed!"

"Don't we all?" someone quipped back. Everyone laughed.

The rest were looking over, nodding, not ridiculing Thomas as he had expected. They only turned away, back to the march. The man switched his attention back to the youth, and Thomas could have sworn a sense of empathy emanated from him as he spoke.

"Aye, I catch yer drift, lad," the man said, his voice filled with a blend of compassion and caution. "But this here ain't the place for ye to linger. Not under any circumstance."

He was probably right, but young Thomas wasn't ready to give up on his journey. He needed to fight, to take up arms for something he believed in. And he believed in it at least because his brother had done so, and his father too.

"My pa perished in the clash of Manassas, and my brother was conscripted," he said, trying to sound as convincing as possible. "So, I want to fight."

The man's eyes widened with sympathy and understanding.

"Mighty sorry to hear that, friend," he offered as he clapped a hand on the lad's shoulder, pausing his steps. "I'm Private Joseph Miller from Cleveland, Ohio."

Thomas extended a hand, also introducing himself, and they began moving again. As Miller and he walked side by side, the private shared with the boy many tales of his life back in Ohio, also about his family and his reason for joining the infantry.

As Thomas listened intently, it felt as if his own brother was recounting his tale. He couldn't help but believe that Miller had gone through similar ordeals, soon also sharing with him his intriguing journey upon arriving at military training, painting for the infiltrator quite a scene.

And the scene came true; in no time, he found they had arrived at a massive line with countless other recruits just as Miller had said, commencing with piles of administrative paperwork and ending with shorn heads and bewildered glances. "Expect to feel very out of place," he had warned. "Oh, and as for my hair, they shaved it all off," he added and chuckled, removing his hat and running his hand through his velveteen hair. "And if ye take this path, they'll do the same to ye. But catch yer breath, friend. We'll march again in a minute."

What? Again? Poor Thomas' thoughts were in disarray. *How can we march again? Surely, this is as far as we'll go for today.*

It already felt as though his stick thin legs were an inch or two shorter, so much hard walking had the group accomplished. He had imagined they might spend the night there, have something to eat and take a rest. But this was no little stopping point, not a rest place.

Thomas looked around; his legs already jittery with nerves; it seemed every word Joseph had spoken was correct. Some of the men were even shedding tears, caught off guard by that same abrupt change Thomas also did not expect.

They were all then herded into the next room, their uniforms awaiting them. From that moment onward, it seemed he had entered a community of men who must have been almost deaf since constant yelling was the only means of communication, offering no moments of respite.

Through this shared adversity, he had to believe they were beginning to forge a bond borne of intimidation, exhaustion, and cold fear, but at the same time, perhaps these sentiments were just Thomas' own; there was no way to know since they did not speak to one another. Even so, he couldn't help but inquire of Joseph, "So, why did you choose to join?"

"Same reason as for most of us, lad. I was raised in a small town," he said. "Opportunities were scarce. I needed a way out and some financial stability. And thus, here I am."

As more and more men from the regiment fell back to join them, they marched on just as he had said. Each soldier showed intrigue in the presence of the young boy who had tagged along, prompting Thomas to explain his reasons once again. They listened attentively, their interest evident, patiently answering Thomas' questions about their mission.

He expected them to tell him to leave, but they welcomed him with open arms instead. As they walked, they also laughed, sharing stories. Were they forming a bond? The men, especially the younger ones, were beginning to feel like cousins, a fond relationship growing, sometimes fueled by respect but most often by banter. They poked fun at Thomas, delighting in the fact he gave back just as he took.

"You think they'll let you enlist with those skinny legs of yours?" one asked.

Thomas didn't take offense. "Hey, I like my chickens' legs," he retorted, laughing. "Anyway, being thin will help me escape the enemy. I'll slide under things and slither out of their grip."

Everyone guffawed. It was what he had been seeking for so long now, all young men together, the "brothers" he had been yearning for. Of course, every so often, his thoughts went to his true brother, the one he hoped to discover again along the way. Where would he be right now?

There was no answer to that; perhaps these boys could help him to pinpoint the places he might be. But the lighthearted atmosphere was interrupted. Soon, the man with stripes gave the order to build a camp for the night. Thomas turned to Private Miller, eager to learn more about the military hierarchy. "What do those stripes mean?" he asked him.

"They mean he's a sergeant, an officer without the privilege of a commission," Miller explained. Seeing the lad's confusion, he continued, "He's the foremost driver under the commanding officer, tasked with leading us and executing commands on the battlefield. The stripes on his sleeve don't come easy; a man must prove himself on the front lines or earn them by years of experience."

Thomas nodded, understanding the importance of such a position. As he glanced at the sergeant, he caught his eye. The sergeant beckoned him over with an intensity that made his heart race.

Thomas' mind raced as he approached the military man, unsure of what he wanted. "Yes, sir?" he asked tentatively. All his new brothers and cousins looked on, and you could have heard a pin drop as they silenced themselves to hear everything the superior was saying to the boy.

It was all too obvious what they were doing.

Someone say something, Thomas thought. *Funny how the place falls as still as a morgue the minute this sergeant wants to talk to me.* The men's silence was pervasive and irritating; he knew exactly what they were doing. Their eyes were boring into him at the same time.

So, there he stood before him, just waiting, feeling small and insignificant in the presence of a man of senior rank. The sergeant studied Thomas briefly, every inch of the lad tensing before the elder man finally asked, "What's your name, boy?" His tone was firm, commanding, yet also not intimidating. At least that was something.

Thomas cleared his throat, nerves threatening to betray him before he responded, "My name is Thomas Adams, Sergeant."

The man's laughter filled the space. Thomas' unease intensified.

"Very well, Thomas Adams," the man started, amusement lacing his words. "What are you doing here? You seem to have become something of a—how can I say this—a *hanger on,* lad. I trust you do have a reason to be here, do you? A proper reason, not just that you like the idea of one day becoming a man."

Everyone laughed, and Thomas did too, but it was awkward. So, Thomas was not considered a man quite yet, and this sergeant had just reminded him of that fact in the most brutal fashion, putting him in his place. Thomas would not let it bother him; joining the regiment would make him into one, and he was sure of it. Still, the unnamed sergeant eyed him, his gaze fixed on his demeanor.

The men around had attempted to look busy in the last few seconds because of their sergeant staring at them harshly too. They now halted their activities once more, their attention fully focused on the conversation between Thomas and the sergeant for a second time. If it were at all possible, then Thomas would have said that everything stilled. In that moment, this sergeant held all the power, his gaze piercing through him.

Summoning his courage, he trembled as he spoke. The words did not come easily, for he had not thought through his reasons in any logical way. "I want to fight, Sergeant. It's—it's all I want."

The sergeant drew back, his eyes wide. "I see. And how old are you, Adams?"

"Old enough to fight, sir." He had failed to answer his superior's question but wanted to get across his point. Now, the sergeant was slowly nodding.

"And you wish to fight because…? What would be your rationale? It is not a decision to take lightly. There is so much a boy can do with his future. War is not the only path."

"I do not take it lightly, sir. And there's nothing else I would like to do. You see, my father died in battle at Manassas, and my brother was drafted. I no longer even know where he is. And that's, um, that's why I want to fight."

At this, the sergeant sighed loudly, plainly exasperated with the youth already.

The sergeant's stern expression didn't waver as he stepped forward, narrowing the distance between the two until they were mere inches apart. For a second, it looked as though he might hit the boy, giving him a clip around the ear. But he did not.

"Bullshit," the sergeant retorted sharply, letting out a snort of derision at the same time. "That's a horrible reason to be here. Boys younger than thee laid their lives beside mine, fighting for a cause. And many are here no more, yet even they had better reasons than those that just escaped your lips. If you want to fight, you will need to come up with reasons more believable than that."

Though a mix of shame, intimidation, and threatened pride pricked at his senses, Thomas remained steadfast. The older man whispered, "Look. If it were in my hands, lad, I'd dispatch ye home forthwith. However, the current terrain is getting perilous. When we arrive in York tomorrow, we shall leave it to the captain to pronounce a verdict. So, kindly trail Private Miller and heed his instructions for the time being. Do you understand, young one?"

Straightening his posture, Thomas responded with a crisp, "Yes, Sergeant!"

As he turned to walk away, he couldn't help but feel a surge of newfound confidence. His voice carried, somehow daring to ask, "What is your name, Sergeant?"

The addressee halted in his steps and turned his head slightly, his eyes meeting Thomas' own. "Sergeant Aust," he replied firmly. "And don't you forget it."

Thomas stood tall, his resolve solidifying in that moment. "Yes, Sergeant," he replied with conviction, watching as the austere man walked away. A sigh of relief escaped his lips, realizing that, for now, he had managed to endure a worse scrutiny. And for some reason, Sergeant Aust was allowing the newcomer to stay; just as the sergeant did not accept the boy's reason for wishing to fight, Thomas did not accept Aust's reason for not sending him home. At least he hoped there was more to it than the man had said, trusting he was giving him a chance.

As he replayed the interaction, his inner voice clamored with doubt and uncertainty. It screamed at him to turn back, to go back home just as Sergeant Aust had suggested.

Aust was probably right. Thomas didn't belong among these men, these soldiers fighting for noble causes while he grappled with his own identity. At that moment, he couldn't help but feel unworthy of their company, so lost and out of place. The heady camaraderie of earlier had dissipated, all the men now getting on with their work and paying Thomas no heed.

Sensing his unease, Private Miller finally nudged the boy gently and offered a dose of sage advice. "Don't mind Sergeant Aust," he reassured. "Every sergeant exists to terrify you, lad. But you'll get used to it. And eventually, you'll learn to respect it. Hell, even to want it, as crazy as that sounds!"

Confusion clouded Thomas' expression as he regarded Miller with wide-eyed uncertainty. Yet Miller simply laughed, his warm tone and his crinkled eyes carrying forward the hint of amusement. "Sergeants ain't all that different from us. They have to show tough love to inspire us to reach our fullest potential. Nothing to fear from him, young 'un."

Though Private Miller's words offered some temporary solace, the feeling of not belonging would continue to gnaw at Thomas. Sergeant Aust had made it painfully clear that he lacked a legitimate reason for being here, and the disapproval in his eyes had left its indelible mark.

However, Private Miller presented a fresh perspective, a glimmer of hope for Thomas in the midst of his self-doubt. "Perhaps, lad, you may not belong among us in the traditional sense," he mused, his voice filled with a gentle understanding. "But then again, maybe you fit right in. Despite all odds, the fact that you're here shows you ain't afraid to fight alongside us."

Thomas pondered his words later while lying in his tent, a realization dawning. Today had been one of fear, challenge, and adventure. It had been uncomfortable, making him feel like an outsider. Yet beneath those layers of uncertainty, he had experienced something powerful, something stirring within. Though the reasons for his presence here remained elusive, the simple fact that he still stood amidst these courageous men held a significance of its own.

For now, that alone was enough.

The sound of movement and clatter outside his tent interrupted his thoughts. He jolted bolt upright, his heart skipping a beat of anticipation. *Is it time already?* It still seemed pitch black outside. A sudden sense of panic gripped at his chest, his heart thumping as if seeking to escape his ribcage. There was nothing to do except to step out of his tent and head straight for the commotion.

He found Private Miller and a few others already up and about, washed and dressed, their faces lighting up with amusement as they turned to greet him. "Morning, boy," one of them called out, a wide grin stretching across his face. "You managed to haul yourself from the cot at last? Sleep well?"

Rubbing his bleary eyes, Thomas replied with a hint of grogginess. "Morning. Not a bad sleep, thanks. But I thought we weren't supposed to move out until sunrise."

The men erupted into laughter, shaking their heads. "Sunrise! Ha! When a sergeant bellows at the break of dawn, it's a clear sign we need to be up and ready," one of them explained. "Consider it one of the unwritten rules around here. You'll soon get the hang of things."

"I'm not even sure I'll stay if it means getting up early," he quipped. The men laughed.

"Typical youthful attitude," one said, and they continued their chores.

In a mixture of foolishness and gratitude to find he was still here, Thomas took a deep breath, steadying himself. Private Miller sauntered up.

"Adams, you'll need to pack up our tent. Think you can manage it alone? I'll be over there, preparing the supply wagon." He pointed.

Eager to prove himself, Thomas responded with newfound confidence, "Okay, I'm on it!"

"Make sure it's neat and follows a system," Miller advised with a wave of the hand.

System? What sort of system?

Thomas was sure he must have looked confused.

"Any system, but it must be an orderly one; do not just bundle it up haphazardly. Everyone accepts you are new, even our sergeant. You won't know how we do things yet, so we won't be expecting miracles. But one thing I can tell you is that when you use your own method to achieve any task, you'll need to ensure it's a good one, borne of sound judgment. That means it must be a tidy, logical system, making the item easy to carry and to store alongside everything else. No loose ends, no bulges, no flopping straps, that sort of thing. Oh, and compact. And you'll need to give everything a good shake for good measure, lad. Many a man has come to grief through insect bites by not checking there is nothing making its home in a tent or bedding. Of course, you will do the men's bedding too, and we cannot afford to be several men down through infections from bites."

He was not expecting a miracle, he'd said. With that interminable list, however, it sure sounded like one. Thomas' eyes glazed over, eyeing the huge tent structure with all its fastened bed rolls and woolen blankets. All the men had tidied their own beds, but everything still needed packing.

In an orderly fashion, he thought. *No bulges. Easy to carry... And what was the rest?*

In that moment, Thomas busied himself alongside his fellow soldiers, undertaking the task to the best of his ability. In a way, it was good for him, and he was enjoying it, a sense of belonging beginning to take root. Though still learning the intricacies of camp life and navigating the myriad of unspoken rules, the opportunity to contribute and play his part was already filling him with deep satisfaction. In these moments of collective effort, he began to glean valuable lessons, immersing himself in what he believed to be the realities of a life as a soldier.

Sergeant Aust's command came brisk and sharp. "Fall in!" he said.

Instantly, Thomas' heart leaped into overdrive as he hurried to join the ranks, aligning himself with the rest of the men who fell into formation, organizing themselves into columns of four. Sergeant Aust's unmistakable voice boomed once more, "Forward march!" and as if bound by an invisible thread, everyone moved forward in perfect unison, their synchronized footsteps resounding. Well, Thomas picked up the pace to match theirs and all was well until they'd been moving for some minutes.

By now, Thomas was trailing behind, a wave of insecurity and tiredness washing over him as he struggled to find his rhythm or tempo. But his shortcomings were the least of his concerns; they were heading toward what looked like a war zone.

Billowing smoke accrued on the horizon, even the oxygen seeming heavy with tension conveying the gravity of the situation.

Pressing on along a winding road, the streams of smoke grew denser, casting an ominous pall over the journey. It became clear that they were drawing near to the Union camp stationed in York, where the events of the impending battle would unfold.

Finally at the entrance to the camp, Thomas stood in awe, beholding a sprawling expanse of white tents stretching endlessly. They had reached their destination, but a question lingered. *What lies ahead?*

Uncertainty gripping his thoughts, Sergeant Aust's voice made itself heard once more, commanding, "Present arms!" The men raised their weapons and stood tall in a powerful display of readiness and resolve. Hindered by his position at the rear, Thomas strained to catch a glimpse of who or what stood before them, commanding such respect.

"Platoon, dismissed!" bellowed the voice.

Thomas nervously approached, taking in the sight of the distinguished officer standing before him. His dark blue single-breasted officer's blouse fit him like a glove, also boasting five gleaming gold buttons and distinct captain rank shoulder boards. His uniform was crisp and immaculate, a testament to his precision and professionalism. Just as Private Miller had instructed Thomas when he'd packed the tent, presentation and neatness mattered. If one day he could present himself just as tidily, then he would truly have become a soldier.

There was something unmistakably distinctive about this man, setting him apart from any regular sergeant. The interactions between the men and the commanding officer exuded an air of formality and respect, revealing the significance of this man's position. He radiated confidence, standing tall with his chest puffed out, a sharp and penetrating gaze surveying the formation and leaving every soldier on edge. Their eyes shifted one to the next, displaying a marked unease.

Private Miller whispered, explaining that Sergeant Aust was the captain's right-hand man, which also was why he seemed to be the only one privileged to talk to him. But then, the captain surprised Thomas by breaking his composure, suddenly smiling wide at something Sergeant Aust had said. Then he turned to look at his young protégé, his smile fading.

Thomas' whole body froze.

"Come here, lad!" he thundered.

What does he want with me now?

Young Thomas rushed to his side, assuming a bolt upright stance, maintaining his composure.

"My name is Captain Miranda, Regiment Commander," the deep voice boomed. He scared Thomas into standing even straighter, intimidating him without even needing to try, watching the would-be soldier trying to steady his nerves.

This imposing man was holding his delicate future in his own hands.

"Sergeant Aust informs me that you have run away from home and have been traveling with the regiment since the train station," Miranda continued. "Would this be correct?"

Sweat trickled down Thomas' back and into his clothes. Confessing his truth was daunting. He met Miranda's steady gaze. "Yes, sir, I did." Then Thomas mused on it. "In fact, I would not call it running away exactly since what happened is—"

"I have neither time nor interest in the finer details. You know there will be a battle here in the coming days," Miranda interjected, abruptly cutting Thomas off. "And this is no place for a young lad like you." His eyes were searching the boys for answers, a frown appearing as the youth only seemed to shrink back into his own skin. "Why are you here, really? This is men's work," Miranda went on, intolerant.

Thomas' fractured past gripped him tightly, the thoughts of returning home or facing life in an orphanage sending equal quantities of shivers down his spine. He mustered all his courage. He would simply tell him the truth. "Sir, to be honest, my parents passed away, and my brother was sent off to fight in the war. It was a case of either joining the regiment or being turned over to an orphanage, and this seemed like the better option."

The captain looked just as unimpressed as Thomas expected, appearing to wait for him to elaborate. But no better reasons or explanations had found their way to Thomas yet. "I, um, I—" He searched his mind for more words, more adequate ones that might impress the senior man more. None came, his mind nothing but a blank slate. And still, Thomas could not help mumbling a fumbled response. "Oh, and I've always wanted—"

"Hush, boy!" Miranda shouted. "You've had your chance. I believe we all get the picture by now, so no need for embellishment. You have nowhere to go and no one to go home to, so you came to my regiment as a last resort! I see."

He seemed so displeased at what he saw as Thomas' inadequacy. Yet the captain was still musing on the responses. Finally, he nodded, adding, "Well, I dare say we have all been there, boy—or many of us have. But is it sufficient reason to take up arms? I would say not, regrettably."

A silence descended, Captain Miranda exchanging a glance with Sergeant Aust, their eyes communicating a taciturn understanding passing between them. Captain Miranda's voice softened with empathy, breaking the tension. "We are sorry to hear about your loss, son."

The would-be recruit's fate hung in the balance then, dismissed to wait anxiously for a decision from the pair. His feet jittered, just about resisting the urge to pace up and down while at the same time, a sticky sweat trailed from his fingertips. He wiped his palms on his trouser thighs, sighing, trembling—everything it was possible to do to show nervousness.

Soon, even his feet joined in, and his heart raced as he looked down at his toes in nervous anticipation as if his boots might come up with a response for him. They didn't, of course, only he locked eyes with Captain Miranda who turned away as the air grew taut with apprehension, pondering his next words. The next outcome would determine the trajectory of Thomas' life, whether infused with new purpose or confined to the shadows of his past. The dreaded orphanage was looming large again, and already, he stood at its gates in his mind, asking to be let in while at the same time, begging they would keep him out of it.

A gruff voice cut through the silence, startling his thoughts.

He looked up, his eyes wider than he believed it possible, to find both a sergeant and Captain Miranda peering down. Sergeant Aust's eyes flickered in disbelief.

He glanced at Miranda, who was evidently still contemplating the youth's fate.

Aust's demeanor seemed to say, *well? What shall I tell the lad?*

Then, with measured words, the captain found some words to say, his voice resonating with a mix of opportunity and caution. "Here's how it will work for you. We happen to be short on a drummer boy, and our campgrounds are in need of resourceful hands. You are not of age to join the fight, nor can I permit such a thing, for your blood would be on my hands if I were to allow it. You will serve here voluntarily, with the option to leave whenever you wish. We cannot provide financial compensation, but we can offer the food and training to help you better yourself."

"And...and if I stay long enough, sir? And if I prove useful enough?" Thomas heard the question escape before it was possible to check it.

"We will see," said Captain Miranda, his lips pressing into a firm line as if displeased to hear Thomas answer back. "If *long enough* and *useful enough,* perhaps we can offer something more when you are of an age."

A certain gratefulness in Thomas was paired with hesitancy to be a drummer.

Drumming? Since when did drumming interest me? And how does that correspond to my wish to become a fighting man, a soldier? Are soldiers ever drummers, or drummers' true soldiers?

He believed not, but what could he know, he who was but a wayward child in their eyes? So, a drummer he would be, whether he liked the notion or not. Otherwise, if Thomas fought against it, they would find him a liability and cast him out, back to where he had come from. That, in his mind, would be a fate worse than meeting his death on any battlefield, beating out a tune on a drum.

"Sir, thank you," Thomas responded, his voice filled with appreciation. "I am willing to do whatever it takes but confess an uncertainty about my abilities to serve as a drummer boy. What about a place in the infantry, like the other fellas?"

In a blink of an eye, the captain responded, "And tell me, have you ever tried to play the drums?"

Thomas looked at Sergeant Aust and then back at Captain Miranda. "No, sir, I have never played the drums. I am not musical and know nothing about it, sir."

Without missing a beat, the captain chuckled and turned. "Sergeant Aust, refresh my memory. When did you learn to build a campsite?"

"Sir, I learned as a young private."

"And how many campsites have you built under my command?" the captain asked.

"Too many to count, sir. Thousands, I dare say."

The captain returned to Thomas and said, "That's right. Sergeant Aust has built so many campsites, he cannot possibly count them all. And you, my lad, shall be heard drumming in camp night and day until we are all verging on deafness and begging for quiet. When you can no longer recall how many times you have practiced or how many times we have pleaded for peace, then shall we say you have tried being a drummer boy and found it not to your particular predilection. All right? Now, please do me a favor by preparing yourself to become our drummer. Training shall commence tomorrow morning at 0700 sharp. Sergeant Aust shall extend to you his aid in obtaining your equipment."

Thomas' pulse pounded in his veins. Oddly, he liked the way the captain had portrayed it, that just by drumming—*his* drumming—it was possible to so influence all the men. "Yes sir!"

The captain walked away, and Sergeant Aust snapped to attention and saluted, leaving Thomas in awe of them both and of the task ahead.

Sergeant Aust's stern voice broke through his thoughts as he watched Captain Miranda's departure. "Thomas," he said, his tone displaying an undercurrent of concern. "We shall fulfill the captain's request, but I shall train you to the highest standards. Any failure to meet those standards may result in your return home. This encampment is no place for a mere boy. I stand by my conviction that we should not be keeping you here."

His words struck a chord within Thomas, a blend of caution and warning deflating his ego that had been soaring somewhere in the clouds at the captain's words. Sergeant Aust was harboring reservations about these decisions, yet he remained a loyal soldier, committed to his duty.

That night, as he lent a hand with campsite duties, his mind buzzed with a whirlwind of thoughts. *Drummer boy? Is this really what I am to be doing?*

Amidst the flurry of concerns and doubts, the respect shown by his fellow soldiers acted as a soothing balm. Word quickly spread of his voluntary commitment, and one by one, they approached, conveying admiration and support.

Their words and gestures served to ease his nerves, but deep down, it was clear that he had an arduous journey ahead. Yet he was determined to meet and exceed Sergeant Aust's expectations, ready to push himself harder than ever before.

As sleep claimed Thomas that night, he understood that his journey had only just begun, embracing the uncertainty with an indomitable spirit.

A Fresh Beat

As Thomas stood outside waiting for Sergeant Aust, the first rays of dawn painted the sky a vibrant shade of orange, casting an ethereal glow upon the campsite.

In his new blue uniform, he still couldn't help but feel like an imposter.

The scratchy wool fabric clung to his skin, devoid of any distinguishing stripes on the sleeves, while the pair of oversized black boots clomped awkwardly with each step, and the task of cinching the belt tightly to hold everything together felt impossible. But it was the drum that left him feeling particularly vulnerable. Its sheer size, towering above him from the waist to knees, seemed only to mock his diminutive stature as if calling out, *ha, little boy! So, you really think you can master me? Why don't you try, and let's see who masters who in this task!*

Its shimmering metallic blue and striking red trim caught the eye, and had it been some other object such as a butterfly or a trinket box, the combination would have made it compelling to his eye. Yet this humongous drum's magnitude and how it glinted only added to his trepidation.

Several men walked by, hollering their praise, their words carrying a blend of jest and respect, "Well done, drummer lad!

Looks good on you!" It was too early to decipher their intent, though Thomas appreciated the acknowledgement regardless. But Sergeant Aust's imminent arrival would undoubtedly complicate matters further.

Just then, someone called out Thomas' name. He instantly snapped to attention, shoulders back and arms rigid at his sides. There was no time for pleasantries as Sergeant Aust wasted none either, his voice cutting through the crisp morning air.

"Right then, you are here to learn, and I am here to teach. Under my tutelage, you will learn all the basics of marching, all right?" He did not wait for a response. "And come afternoon, we shall begin to add the drum to the equation. Prepare yourself for rigorous drilling!" There was a long way to go before the young drummer boy could begin to master the art of drumming, but he was willing to put in the work.

Sergeant Aust fulfilled all his promises, drilling the lad on the fundamentals of marching. They started with simple movements, such as standing in line and executing left and right turns. There was more to it than ever Thomas had considered before, but gradually, they progressed to more intricate maneuvers. With each step, Aust pushed Thomas to his limits, instructing him on maintaining formation and ensuring that his feet moved in perfect synchrony with the other soldiers' own. It was a challenging endeavor, leaving him stumbling through the initial attempts. However, fueled by a burning inner fire, Thomas funneled all his energy into getting it right.

One thing had already become clear, and it was that around here, there was no room for claims of *I don't know how,* or *I need a rest.* Whatever the task, however great or small, a soldier needed to execute his work flawlessly and to the death if need be, or so it felt to Thomas as he hit that infernal taut leather for the thousandth time.

Despite his stern demeanor, Sergeant Aust's enthusiasm for his progress was palpable. Thomas soon discovered that he possessed a keen eye for detail, refusing to let him succumb to frustration or give up. He pushed him to persist, correcting his posture and technique until his movements began to exhibit a semblance of proficiency, a smoothness, certain strikes coming naturally.

Confidence grew within Thomas, forged through sweat and perseverance, and he allowed the true value of the training to permeate.

As the sun descended, Sergeant Aust delivered his final instructions in a tone carrying a mixture of pride and expectation. "Master Adams, you must continue to practice these motions until they are ingrained in you, young fellow."

Thomas nodded in understanding, fully aware that the training was far from over. Yet in that moment, the Sergeant had also bestowed upon him a sense of purpose and a burgeoning pride in his uniform. It was astonishing, even to Thomas, to note how different it felt to have become a part of something, a would-be vital part of a band of men to which he had been yearning to belong.

In the ensuing days, their training intensifying, they moved on from the principles of marching to the basic techniques of drumming. Thomas was now into the skill set for which the army had a use for him, and for this, he was excited, even if it was not the fighting action for which he had hoped.

Each session continued to unmask the depth of his shortcomings, but he would not have anticipated anything other. The early self-consciousness was thankfully waning by now; after making a plethora of pitiful errors over and over, his skin was gradually toughening against all the criticisms, and soon, he could tell by a mere glance at Aust's face whether he was about to make him repeat the exercise.

On occasion, Thomas ran through it again before the Sergeant even managed a word. And Thomas noted something else, too, which was that Aust was never belittling him, never mocking, only correcting, demanding he try again. He decided Aust was a good master under whose tutelage to learn, someone he trusted and who had earned his respect.

For his part, Sergeant Aust would have known the magnitude of the task before him, no doubt observing in the drummer a woeful inadequacy. They began with the fundamentals such as mastering the grip, Thomas familiarizing himself with the various positions and comprehending the intricacies of different beats.

Sergeant Aust demonstrated each type of beat, ranging from the simple "paradiddle" drum roll to the more complex "flam" drumming technique. Thomas struggled initially; his drumming was inconsistent, greatly lacking the required strength and tempo.

His arms soon felt fit to break, the elbow joints inflamed, a burning sensation also setting into his weak and skinny wrists that had never received any form of exercise before.

Well, being in the regiment should build me up, he said to himself in silent thought. *Perhaps this isn't the way I wished for it to happen, but still, it will build my arms if nothing else.*

Then came another intrusive thought. How would he end up looking if his arms gained musculature and his legs remained undeveloped? No matter. It was what it was. He was stuck with it, the little drummer boy that he was set to become.

As the days passed, Sergeant Aust continued to push him to do better, drilling him on the basic beats until they were nearly perfect. Gradually, Thomas increased the tempo and slowly gained control over the drumsticks, his movements becoming more fluid.

Sergeant Aust was pleased with his progress, praising his willingness to learn.

Despite the initial hurdles, Thomas began reveling in the art of drumming, relishing the challenge of striking the right beats at the right time. With each passing day, his confidence surged, and he was finally beginning to believe in his own ability to play the drums. By the end of the week, he even mustered the courage to perform a short piece for Sergeant Aust.

The beats resounded with precision; each movement was executed with measured intent. Sergeant Aust beamed with such obvious pride as if the boy were his own son, witnessing the transformation before him as Thomas marched off, the resounding echoes of the drums filling the campsite.

As the sun dipped below the horizon, casting long shadows the full length of the landscape, Sergeant Aust delivered his fast instructions in a voice filled with gravitas. "Your training is complete, lad. Tomorrow morning at sunrise, you will sound reveille and assembly. The captain wants the formation to rehearse all battle formation movements, so ensure you get a good night's sleep and are ready to execute."

Thomas' stomach fell to the ground. *One day of training isn't enough for me to be ready. I'll fail and look like a fool in front of everyone! My nerves will go to pieces, and they'll all laugh at me.*

That old shyness was back with a vengeance, cajoling him, howling in laughter at his anxiety.

Maybe Sergeant Aust saw his fear then because he turned to him and placed a hand on his shoulder. The warmth of it seeped through his jacket, but Aust's face was stern. He was about to deliver a reprimand, though a warmhearted one.

"Lad, it's plain to see you have doubts in yourself, but let me say one thing. We all start off the same, so even if the men laugh at you, even if you drop a beat or two, the important thing is to carry on and push through it. I don't expect you to make it through the entire day either. Push yourself and do what you can. That is the essence of doing your best for the regiment. The practice is not the end point. The end point is to drum for the regiment."

With that, the man nodded and strode off, leaving his words resounding in Thomas' head. They pleased him, almost moving him to a show of emotion he did not want to allow free. The worries were all still there, but somehow, Sergeant Aust had also instilled a sense of anticipation and eager excitement alongside them all.

"Sergeant Aust, I owe you," he whispered. "And I shall endeavor to do you proud in the morning. Wait and see."

And with that, he made a solemn promise to himself that this would be the drumming performance of his young life. He wanted so dearly to bring pride to his sergeant.

All this had been Aust's way of reassuring him that he could do it, and it seemed to have been effective, but there wasn't much time to read into it. Thomas still had camp details to do, followed by yet more drum practice. Up until this juncture, none of the men had begged him to stop his drumming, and that meant the boy had to work harder at it until they were tired of hearing every repetitive beat, covering their ears.

Anyway, Thomas must have recorded how fast he finished his camp details that night, running from preparing food and cleaning dishes, leaving a dust cloud behind his steps. As most men were asleep, he couldn't use the drum at this hour, so he practiced by beating on a brown leather journal over near the campfire. A smile broke out across his face when he heard from somewhere nearby, "Thomas, you sure are earning your keep around the camp. Are you going to enlist or what?"

He turned in the direction of the voice to see Private Miller, several men with him. "I appreciate that. Captain says I'm still too young, so I can only volunteer as the drummer boy."

The words carried a disappointed tone.

"Hmm, well, you never know," said a different voice. "I heard a few units are out there with boys under eighteen. Not sure how they did it, but is enlisting something you even want to do?"

Most of the men looked at him, interested to observe how the youngest of them would answer. Their faces had been those of strangers several days ago, but now they had all grown familiar and dear to him in their own right. They had all bonded, sometimes through the pure misery of exhaustion and hard work, but they also reveled in their many laughs and conversations to pass the time. Weirdly, this all reminded Thomas of when his family had been all together.

Looking at Private Miller and the men, he responded, "I never thought I would say this, but yes, I want to enlist." The men started cheering, embracing him and lifting him high onto their shoulders until Sergeant Aust yelled out, "Keep quiet! May I remind you, men, you are not children!"

They quietly snickered to themselves as they slunk away, leaving the campfire to head to their respective tents.

As Thomas lay down just a little later, his mind wandered from one thought to another, fluctuating between anticipation and worry. Oddly, his musings were turning more and more to his dear brother Henry, who had departed months ago to join the war efforts. The distance between them felt insurmountable, and Thomas still did not know where Henry was in the world.

On most days, the strain of all the marches and his incessant drumming and practice kept Thomas tired and preoccupied, so why had all these intrusive thoughts been invading his head lately?

A persistent unease settled in his heart. What was Henry experiencing out there? Had he encountered the horrors of war?

Shall Henry and I ever cross paths again?

He also thought how it would be impossible to receive notification, should Henry become maimed or killed as their father had been. Now, there was no one back at home in their family's cottage. How would he ever receive news if something did happen to his brother? Would a letter arrive at a vacated family home?

Then again, perhaps it was to his advantage that he would not know—unless, of course, poor Henry were to be sent back wounded from the front, only to find an abandoned house. That thought struck Thomas out of the blue, filling him with horror and palpitations.

Throughout the night, his mind drifted into daydreams, envisioning a life in which Henry stood by his side once more. Thomas yearned to hear his stories, to learn about the people he had met along his way and the battles he had fought. Though separated, his presence was lingering in his thoughts these days, a constant reminder of the unbreakable bond they had shared as siblings. Under the pressure of the regiment's activities, there had barely been time to think of the past or to miss anyone.

At first, it was exactly what Thomas had needed, since the wound of losing Henry as well as his parents had been all too raw. But now, somehow, Henry's face and his voice were creeping back into Thomas' mind night and day, an all-pervading thought as he settled better into his new life as the regiment's drummer boy. It wasn't a thought he wished to push away, and it was painful not knowing anything about his brother's whereabouts or activities since he had left their home. But at the same time, it all unsettled him deeply.

For one thing, Henry didn't even know about the devastating loss of their mother, and the more time that passed, the more upset Thomas became, feeling he was somehow hiding a terrible secret from the person he adored more than anything else in life, even though there was nothing he could do about it.

He was aware of how the war bore down on him too, questions about its worth plaguing his young mind. The sheer magnitude of death and devastation the conflict was causing left him questioning its very purpose.

More than anything, he was fearing the day when news would arrive, delivering the dreaded announcement of Henry's fall in battle or a life-altering injury. The ache of missing him and their family was a constant companion, tugging at his heartstrings. The one thing for which he could be grateful, however, was that it did not distract him when at work.

The moment he began drumming, the beat was everything and the only thing, no space in his mind for anything else, no room for complexity or tangled musings.

Pushing aside the memories and worries of the past, Thomas rolled over in an attempt to find solace in sleep before the momentous day ahead.

However, the anticipation and stress robbed him of rest.

***

The next morning, Thomas was the first awake in the camp.

Hastily, he donned his uniform that he had pressed and made pristine the night before, as always, and snatched up his drum, rushing toward the designated flat area.

As the bright orange hues of the rising sun peeked over the tree line, he began to play *reveille,* the familiar rhythms echoing through the morning air. The first figure he spotted, dressed immaculately in his uniform, was Captain Miranda. It was evident that he had not wasted a moment, for he emerged from his tent with an air of purpose. Swiftly, young Thomas saluted him, his voice filled with respect. "Good morning, Captain."

The captain's response was curt, as expected, but focused on acknowledging the greeting.

"Good morning to you," he replied. "Now, sound the assembly for the men."

Thomas beat his drum, pleasantly surprised that he had it to a fine art, at least in his own opinion. In the distance, he witnessed the men springing into action, running and forming themselves into precise formations centered around the commanding presence of Captain Miranda.

At the front, Sergeant Aust saluted, his voice resonating with authority. "Good morning, sir. All men present and accounted for."

Returning the salute, Captain Miranda addressed the assembled soldiers, his voice booming with authority. "Attention, soldiers! Today, we shall focus our training on the maneuvers of marching and firing battle positions." His words carried weight, drawing the attention of every man present. "Some of you may wonder why we dedicate an entire day to this practice. News has reached us that General Lee and his Confederate troops are a mere two-day ride from Gettysburg."

The excitement in the eyes of the men was palpable, their solid commitment to the cause evident. The captain's voice grew even more resolute as he continued.

"As the regiment positioned closest to the area, we are to set forth tomorrow and intercept General Lee before he lays claim to the Potomac and pursues the acquisition of Harrisburg, Pennsylvania." The significance of the task at hand resonated with each soldier, their duty to protect crucial territory and supplies, honoring President Lincoln.

Everything became very real at that moment. The captain turned and looked at Thomas, knowing this would mean something to the drummer boy. Thomas' thoughts moved to memories of his family, Henry, and the people he knew there. This war had broken his family, but it became even more real knowing how many lives would be affected if they failed. Everyone knew it, and they didn't waste any time getting to it, stopping only twice that day for quick hydration and food breaks.

The tensions were high as each man hurried to prepare and rehearse his field tactics.

Thomas was attached to the captain's side the entire day. He would order a command, and Thomas drummed, saying only, "Yes, sir."

Several times, he messed up, but Captain Miranda quickly gave feedback, and they pressed on. Despite the stakes, Thomas remained focused, never allowing the pressure and stress to show, and the captain was the same, calm and collected as he commanded his men. His demeanor and focus set the tone for everyone, and all the men did their best to mirror him.

Everyone was exhausted, but they had a clear purpose for the next day, all one hundred of them to march three hours east to join the Army of the Potomac led by Major General Meade.

In the morning, Thomas sounded reveille and assembly as the entire company with supplies started their march. He walked to the left of the captain and Sergeant Aust, providing cadence occasionally to keep the men in step but, more importantly, awake.

The time slowly passed, and everyone grew restless and anxious. Along with their march, several other Union companies moved to Gettysburg, and Thomas found it interesting to discover how there were so many different units with missions and orders. One of the companies was an artillery unit with red stripes on their sleeves, another a cavalry unit with yellow stripes.

The captain and Sergeant Aust explained how the battle would be organized and the purpose of each unit. It was overwhelming, but Thomas noticed how he was becoming enthralled by all the moving parts. The captain had ordered the company to move at ease, which kept the formation integrity but allowed the men to talk at the same time. Sergeant Aust seemed to be using the opportunity to keep the men motivated.

"Men, we're going to get those damn Confederates out of Gettysburg so we can go home and eat a decent meal. I want to play some cards while I eat some damn good cornbread." The men laughed, bringing up topics of other foods, women, and other things for which they were fighting.

Captain Miranda looked at Thomas.

"Tell me, Adams. How do you like your new role as our drummer boy?"

"Captain, it's growing on me, I reckon. In the beginning, I was all jittery, but now I see how crucial it is and what justifies its necessity."

The captain kept his head looking straight ahead, but Thomas could see him smirk.

"Very well, I knew you'd change thy mind, lad. At first, it might seem uneasy to deal with such an immense and powerful instrument, but I promise, in time, it shall transpire as easily as apple pie. You might even start craving it the same way, believe it or not."

He had a good point. Thomas' life back home before this had pretty much revolved around school and home. Never in a million years had he expected to be playing the drums, let alone marching to fight the Confederates. Now, his daily drumming stilled his disquieted heart, bringing an inner peace that was otherwise hard to find. So, what the captain had said was right. Thomas was already craving his drumming in the way a long-distance runner craved the motion of his feet on the road and the wind through his hair.

The captain looked at him as a cool breeze graced their hot and sweaty bodies.

"The men and I have grown fond of thy presence in the camp, lad. You have earned their admiration, and I have been informed time and time again that you are hankering to enlist. Is there any truth to this, lad?"

Thomas didn't hesitate to respond with gusto, looking forward to the future instead of the past for the first time in a very long while. He knew the answer. "Yes, without a doubt. I want to be here. Not just because I don't want to go to an orphanage but because I also respect the men here. I respect everything for which the regiment stands, and all that it does."

"All *that it does?*" questioned Miranda. He peered at Thomas, quizzical, as if Thomas was expected to correct himself. It left the drummer floundering; what had he said that was amiss?

"I, I don't follow, sir," he offered.

"You said all that *it* does. Do you not mean that you respect all that *we do?* You are a part of something now. You belong in the regiment."

A flush claimed Thomas' cheeks, overcome by a sense of pride.

"I meant all *that we do,* sir. Thank you, sir." He really meant it and struggled to hold back tears. "Thank you, sir." And the young drummer puffed out his chest, for the first time feeling he truly belonged here, conducting his essential task just the same as everyone else.

The captain didn't look surprised to see his protégé's reaction to the praise.

"Well said. And thank you too; you may not realize how important your drumming is for the morale of the men. Concentrate on beating those drums and gathering knowledge, and everything shall pan out smoothly for you in due course."

Thomas smiled excitedly as the ground vibrated from the men's presence, marching around the bend of a hill with several tall trees. Suddenly, there it was. Gettysburg.

During the next several hours, the men set up camp as the captain had to report to an officer assembly to receive their orders. He had asked Thomas to attend with him, so they quickly moved toward the massive tent at the top of the hill.

Stepping through its entrance, the structure having been set up for the officer assembly, a sense of awe and excitement stirred in the drummer boy.

The space was filled with Union officers of all ranks from captains to generals, each focused intently on the dashing figure standing confidently at the head of the gathering. This, he learned, was General Daniel Sickles, the commander of the Third Corps and one of the most respected leaders in the Union Army. As the two made their way through the crowd, Thomas could feel his heart racing with anticipation, eager to hear the general's explanation of the Battle of Gettysburg strategy that would help lead the Union to victory. They listened intently as General Sickles explained the principles of the Fishhook Strategy, pointing to a map of the terrain that would soon become the battlefield. Thomas watched in awe, the general expertly describing the Union's positioning and tactics, outlining the strategic advantages of the high ground.

As he listened to the formidable man's commanding voice and watched his confident gestures, he couldn't help but feel a sense of wonder and admiration for this fierce and determined leader, so dedicated to his country and his men.

The Fishhook Strategy was based on the idea that their forces could use the area's natural topography to their advantage. The general planned to have the Union Army positioned along Cemetery Ridge, a high ground comprising a range of hills offering an excellent vantage point over all the surrounding countryside.

The ridge was shaped like a fishhook, its curved end pointing toward the Confederate Army that had taken up its own position on Seminary Ridge, directly opposite.

The idea was that the Union Army would be utilizing Cemetery Ridge as their anchor point, their forces stretching out along the "hook" toward the ends of the Confederate line. This would allow them to hold their high ground, thus forcing the Confederates to attack uphill, a difficult task that would wear them down before they could even reach Union lines.

The men were also responsible for defending the Union line's southern end, the fishhook's most vulnerable point. Sickles recognized the importance of this position and began fortifying the area with trenches and artillery. As the tent broke into groups discussing the overall strategy, Captain Miranda and young Thomas approached General Sickles. Miranda's face was creased with concern.

"Begging your pardon, General, but I'm mighty anxious about our location on the far south end of the fishhook formation," Captain Miranda said. "Should the Confederates deploy multiple divisions, we might get cut off from additional resources and have to await backup for hours, despite holding the upper hand on the topographical front."

General Sickles listened thoughtfully. "Captain, I hear your worries; we just can't yield this location. It stands as a vital part of our overall plan here at Gettysburg. We must firmly grasp this ground by hook or crook, and I know I can count on you and your men to accomplish it."

Captain Miranda nodded, accepting the general's explanation.

Thomas didn't fully understand the general's rationale, but the captain was bound to explain it all later. The captain joined the Third Corps, planning discussions attentively, understanding their role, and knowing the battle ahead would be fierce.

Several hours of planning and coordination ensued until about midday.

With a commanding voice, General Sickles then dismissed all the officers in the tent to prepare for the first day of battle on the following day, reminding them of the importance of staying focused and vigilant in facing danger.

"Tomorrow will commence the onslaught that shall determine the destiny of our grand nation," he said. "We gotta combat everything, not only for ourselves, but also for the sake of our land's tomorrow and those who reside herein."

As the officers filed out of the tent, they were filled with renewed motivation to carry them through the long, arduous days ahead.

Walking back to camp, the captain discussed their position at the southernmost point of the fishhook, candidly expressing his concerns about the risk and danger it would entail. Despite his concerns about their position, however, he clarified that they had to do everything possible to hold the ground and prevent the Confederate forces from breaking their lines.

Thomas looked up at Captain Miranda, confusion apparent on his face.

"All said and done, why do we have to toe the line and follow the general's commands?" Thomas asked. "Why can't we just do what we think is best?"

Captain Miranda knelt so that he was at eye level with Thomas. "It ain't about our perceptions of what's valuable, I tell ye," he explained. "It's about staying in line, following directives during collaborative combat. The general's strategic big picture surpasses our limited capabilities, and he knows what's needed to emerge victorious in this battle. We must place our faith in his guidance and endeavor to execute his commands to the hilt."

As the captain spoke, Thomas was listening intently, hanging onto every word. He could see the sincerity and passion in the captain's eyes, making it clear the young drummer was in the presence of a true leader. Thomas pondered on his words for a moment before nodding in understanding. Right now, this all left him in no confusion that being a soldier wasn't just about being brave or skilled in battle, but also about taking direction, working together, and being an intrinsic, undeniably essential part of something far greater than himself.

The captain began addressing the regiment on what they had planned. In the background, other units were audible, cheering and preparing as word was received that the Confederates were near. Captain Miranda stood tall and strong as he made his address. Everyone gathered around him, listening intently as he spoke about their fighting strategy, explaining that they would be holding the southernmost point of the fishhook, a crucial strategic position in the efforts to defeat the enemy. It was certain to be a difficult and dangerous task, but Captain Miranda urged his men to stay focused and work together.

He stressed the importance of unity.

"And remember, we can achieve anything if we stay true to our goals and remain willing to work together. The more we fragment ourselves and our stance, the more any enemy can break our defense. The more broken we are, the more cracks our strategy holds, cracks through which our enemy infiltrates. So, men, there shall be no cracks in our defenses, no differences in what we think will work or what we must do. We stand strong, united, always cohesive so that our enemy sees no weakness, no flaws and no fragmentation in us.

"Remember, we are all fighting for a common cause and will only have a chance to succeed if we fight as a team. Be brave and stay focused on the objective, confident we can hold this important territory. Because we can—and we shall."

With that, his regiment's men were all fired up, resolute, determined to a point where an excitement buzzed and hummed, an electrifying sensation that would keep the men alert and awake for most of the night to come.

As the night wore on and pitch darkness claimed the terrain around, they settled to sleep, still agitated. Each soldier was anxious about the impending battle and excited to prove his worth, all knowing they had to stay strong and focused if they were going to succeed.

***

Despite a profound battle weariness that had already settled itself deep in their bones, the men all rose early the next day, gathering their gear and moving into position on the southernmost point of the fishhook. Captain Miranda's words echoed as they prepared for the upcoming battle.

Each man was in no doubt they all had to work together; their minds trained on holding this territory. They gazed far into the distance, preparing themselves for what was to come, a resolute silence descending over everyone. It was the rallying cry of the captain that inspired them, instilling in each soldier—and one drummer—the requisite courage to face whatever the day may bring.

A Mustang is Born

As the regiment stood on the battlefield, the sound of the drums grew more intense.

Adrenaline coursed through the men's veins as they locked eyes with the Confederate Army across the expanse. The scorching sun issued its unforgiving glare, illuminating the determined faces of their foes.

Formidable they appeared, a seemingly endless line of Confederate soldiers, artillery poised for action. Tension crackled, charging the atmosphere with an electric energy.

The Union's men stood staunch and determined, awaiting the command to charge, all hearts in synchrony with the rapid rhythms of the drums.

Louder the drums beat, driving them forward, the relentless thump echoing the pounding in the men's chests. Every soldier stood tall, braced for an imminent clash, eyes fixed unmoving upon the enemy. The moment's intensity held them captive, an unbreakable focus gripping their souls.

Time hung in suspense as both armies poised for the impending clash. Then, as if swallowed by the void, the drums ceased their seemingly unending cadence. The sudden stillness reverberated, a deafening silence enveloping the battlefield.

Each man held his breath, suspended in anticipation, awaiting the battle cry that would ignite the fray. Only the whispers of the wind through the trees and the gentle rustle of soil beneath their boots broke the silence, a prelude to the tempest about to be unleashed.

Thomas stood beside the captain, his heart pounding with anticipation. The brief pause was caught there, hanging in a stagnant and palpable tension before the captain bellowed, "Forward!"

Without hesitation, the drummer boy unleashed every ounce of strength upon the drums, its resounding beats marking the charge of the first wave of men. In a whirlwind of gunfire and clashing blades, the regiment of the Union Army collided head-on with the Confederate Army.

The drums thundered, keeping pace with the chaotic rhythm of the battle itself. There was soon an overbearing clamor of men shouting and cannons roaring, a cacophony of war as the two armies fought ferociously for supremacy. Amidst the turmoil, the Union resolve burned fiercely, driving them forward with unyielding rage and fury. The battlefield became a maelstrom of violence and mayhem, every thought consumed by the relentless combat unfolding.

Under Captain Miranda's leadership, they traversed the fields of Gettysburg, feeling the nervous energy emanating from every soldier. Outnumbered and outgunned, they now relied solely on their determination to claim victory. Yet Captain Miranda's ready confidence in his men shone through, knowing they would not falter, having undergone rigorous training.

As the men held their ground, the thunderous symphony of gunfire and cannon blasts shook the terrain, sending a chilling shiver down each man's spine. Nevertheless, they each fought on, urging their comrades forward with resounding shouts. The battle quickly escalated into a furious frenzy, the ground trembling beneath their feet as explosions rocked the field.

Smoke and dust veiled the scene, obscuring the horrors beginning to unfold. Men screamed and fell, each individual loss striking at the captain's heart.

Amidst the chaos, drummer boy Thomas Adams struggled to keep pace, but Captain Miranda never abandoned him. The Confederate Army pressed them, the Union's grip on the ground starting to slip. In the critical moment, Captain Miranda entrusted him with the call for reinforcements. Yet, even as Thomas sounded the call, fate intervened, causing the boy to lose his footing and crash to the ground. It was then that tragedy seized its chance and struck.

The captain, rushing to the aid of his drummer, was struck with a bullet in the chest.

He crumpled to the earth, his lifeblood staining the grass as his horrified gaze met the scene. The battle raged on, an overwhelming painting of gunpowder and vibrant fresh blood that spurted in fountains from severed arteries before ebbing to meandering rivulets, trickling into the ground.

The soldiers' cries and shouts accosted the air and the fields, drowning out all other sounds. Captain Miranda had somehow made it to his feet again but now gasped, stumbling backward, his hand clutching at his wound. His eyes widened in shock and agony, beginning to roll back as he surveyed his men, but the all-consuming roar of battle rendered them oblivious to his injury.

Racing to his side, trembling with fear and adrenaline, Thomas knew he must fight to save his captain's life. He cried out for help, but amidst the chaos, his voice was lost. The captain's breathing was growing more labored by this time, his grip on Thomas' arm weakening. Desperately, the drummer pressed his hand against the big man's chest, seeking to stem the flow of blood, but his efforts proved futile. The wound was grave, and life was slipping through his drummer's fingers. Tears streamed down Thomas' young face as he held him close, his body wracked with sobs. But Captain Miranda's voice, barely a whisper, reached Thomas' ears as he spoke his final words. "Lad, do not mourn for me. My life has been all that I have wished for, and in winning this battle—as I know you shall—I shall have lived it to the fullest. Keep fighting until you, too, find what you seek."

And with that, he was gone, his eyes wide now, staring—unseeing—at the sky.

Thomas' fat tears, falling onto the captain's uniform, faded into insignificance, drowned out by the relentless roar of battle. As he wiped away his tears, the battle pressed down even more, the deafening gunfire and wheezing cannonballs leaving him dizzy with fear. Yet, amidst the chaos, a stirring surged within the young man, an unyielding pursuit to make a difference. Rising to his feet, he surveyed the enemy lines, focusing on their vulnerable flanks.

Summoning every ounce of energy, Thomas beat his drum with a resolute, steady rhythm. At first, his efforts went unnoticed, also drowned out by war's cruel cacophony. But gradually, his music began to penetrate the tumult, weaving its way into the hearts of those around. Soldiers turned their heads, their eyes searching for the source of the beat until they found it. In other words, they found Thomas, spurred on by him.

Responding to the pulsating beat, his comrades rallied with renewed purpose and resolve. Their steps quickened, propelled by the energy infused by his music. Pride surged within Thomas as he witnessed their advancement. Then, like a gust of hope, the sounds of approaching reinforcements reached everyone's ears. Their comrades had arrived in formidable numbers, ready to join the fray. Together, they charged toward the enemy lines, the huge drum resonating with thunderous intensity, attempting to match the fervor of the Union's charging soldiers.

The symphony of musket fire and booming cannons engulfed them all, but the Union's drummer boy remained steadfast, never missing a beat. The power of his music coursed through the ranks, igniting their spirits, unyielding. The battle raged on, but with the bolstered strength of reinforcements, they gained the upper hand.

In a blur of motion, the Confederate lines faltered, and the Union soldiers surged forward again, closing in on their position. Victory was within reach, a shimmering prize beckoning. Tears streaming down his face, Thomas would not stop, still beating his drum as its rhythm echoed the command that Captain Miranda would have given.

Cheers of victory soon began to sound as the Union forces finally pushed the Confederates back. Embracing one another, tears of joy mingling with their sweat-stained faces, the soldiers celebrated their hard-fought triumph. The end, after enduring so much, was finally in sight.

Yet, as the clamor subsided, a solemn realization swept across the battlefield, the recognition that Captain Miranda lay lifeless. The soldiers' valiant leader, the very embodiment of courage, had fallen. The gravity of the loss struck each man with an intensity beyond words, tears streaming down their faces as they clustered around his lifeless form.

In that poignant moment, their hearts spilling over with grief, their eyes turned to Thomas standing amidst them, drum still in hand. They recognized that he had led them to victory, stepping into the captain's shoes, guiding them through the darkest of moments. With a mix of tears, pride, and gratitude, they approached, embracing him tightly, patting and slapping his back. In turn, they surged forward to thank the boy for shouldering the burden of leadership, for channeling the captain's spirit, and for leading them to the triumphant outcome in which they now reveled as a collective. A sense of pride and accomplishment welled up in him, but there was no real victory in any of this, not for the Union's drummer boy.

The loss of the captain overshadowed it. He had done his best to honor the valiant man's memory and help bring victory to the Union. But beneath it all, a terrible sadness reigned.

The Union Army had just lost one of its finest men, an honorable man, someone who had cared for him too. There were not many such men in this world. In that second, Thomas thought of his brother, too busy to ponder on Henry's fate much lately. He wondered where he was right at this moment and if he had a captain just as good as Miranda.

Suddenly, there were footsteps, and as he looked up, it was Sergeant Aust approaching.

The two looked at each other without saying a word. His face was serious, but it was clear that he was moved by what the drummer boy had just accomplished.

After an awkward pause, he finally spoke.

"Son, the captain was spot on about you. I could never have fathomed it, but how ye fought on and effectively led us was awe-inspiring. Ye be much more than a mere drummer boy; let it be known, ye be kin to us all."

These words took Thomas aback, but his heart swelled. He looked up at Sergeant Aust wide-eyed, aware that for the first time, he was seeing his drummer as a comrade in arms, as a soldier who had fought alongside him, not as a young boy with nowhere to go and for whom some random job had needed to be found to keep him from getting under everyone's feet.

"I learned a lot from the captain," Thomas said in a low voice, still hushed by the loss of a great man whose blood was setting to a deep rust red on the soil. "And he inspired me to do what I did. But I couldn't have done it without the help and support of my fellow soldiers, including you, Sergeant."

Sergeant Aust nodded, and for a second or two, they stood there just looking at each other. At that moment, their respect for each other was palpable, the awareness that they had both fought for a greater cause only deepening the sentiment. There was no difference in rank or status between them anymore, not in this moment anyway. They were only two men on a battlefield, sharing the same aims, breathing the same iron-laden air, moving to the same drumbeat.

The aftermath of Captain Miranda's death and the following victory at Gettysburg proved to be a somber and emotional time for all of the regiment's soldiers. Several days passed, and they had lost many comrades, yet simultaneously, no one could deny they had achieved a significant victory over the Confederate forces.

This loss reminded Thomas yet again of his family.

Momentarily lost, he stood in the middle of the camp as Sergeant Aust approached. "Hey lad, just got word of a new captain coming to us in a few days as we embark on a long march toward Vicksburg, Mississippi."

Thomas' breath caught in his throat at those words. The feelings of being left behind consumed him; Captain Miranda and he had shared a common bond, but a new captain would surely just consider him a boy who was inexperienced and, in the way, a risk to the regiment.

And why should he expect anything other? It was not usual for *hangers on*—as the captain had earlier put it—to be accommodated or tolerated, not even for a day. Just as he'd said, there was no place for a boy in battle. By now, the young drummer had lost count of the days the men had allowed him to stay at their sides, and he felt sure he had earned his place here, but why would any new senior see him as anything but a liability?

"What about me? Will the new captain let me be his drummer boy? If not, will I be sent back home to an orphanage?" Thomas nervously said. In his mind, he was already packing his few sparse possessions into a wooden crate to send home.

Aust actually smiled, a rare sight to behold. "I figured you would ask that, young 'un."

He handed Thomas a letter in Captain Miranda's handwriting. The drummer took a seat on a small stool, intent on reading every word without wavering. Yet he delayed.

For a few moments, he rubbed his thumb and forefingers across the shabby thin paper, then stared at the letter, pursing his lips in uncertainty. He was very unsure of what would be inside that envelope, his hand quivering on opening and reading the flimsy sheets.

Inside were a number of earlier detailed messages from Captain Miranda to his superiors, each one requesting that they please consider allowing Thomas Adams, drummer boy, to join the Union Army, not just as their prized and irreplaceable drummer but this time, as an enlisted soldier. "The Adams boy has many times shown his fabric," said one. "And a better or more loyal and determined young man we shall never encounter, not in ten years and a day." Another proclaimed, "This drummer is the heartbeat of our regiment. Let this be known far and wide." And finally, in the last letter prior to his grievous end, the captain had written, "This young man would lay down his life for any of us."

He had included personal testaments from the regiment's men, as well as justifications. Furthermore, a parent or guardian could grant an enlistment for volunteers under eighteen, the letters insisted, stressing that if the boy had no guardian, it would be a sorry loss indeed.

Tears rolled down the boy's cheeks, dripping onto the paper, but as quickly as the tears fell, Thomas tried to brush them away from the letter lest they should smudge that precious ink; it felt akin to washing away the captain's blood, wasting the last small vestiges of his life force.

He turned the page and scanned it, recoiling in sudden surprise, his eyes wide.

He looked up, startled. "But…this…this is my brother Henry's signature on the enlistment paperwork," he began, his voice trembling, and his hand jittering. "I would know this signature anywhere, even before reading the name. He signed and dated it nine whole days ago. He has known where to find me all this time?"

He was stunned; should he feel good about this, or upset that his brother had not sent any personal missive?

Sergeant Aust grabbed Thomas' shoulder, no doubt seeing a look of confusion flitting across the boy's features. "Lad, I promise you, we had no idea, and no doubt your brother did not wish to let it be known in case it should bring any sense of added pressure or stress to bear. But I swear that Captain Miranda said Henry Adams was smiling a most peculiar grin from ear to ear."

Thomas beamed.

Sergeant Aust went on, "Look, lad. The captain had no intention of raising your expectations, so he worked on it in secret, keeping it close to his chest, you understand. And until your signature graces these papers, the decision still lies with you. You are, of course, under no obligation to—"

He needed not say more because in one swift gesture, young Thomas Adams' hand reached for the fountain pen that had been languishing in Aust's hand. "Here, please pass the pen to me, sir," he said. "If it's all right with you, I would like to sign right away." His eyes sparkled with eagerness and joy.

His brother and Captain Miranda had already signed the enlistment paperwork. Sure enough, only one place remained for a signature.

His own.

PART TWO:
AN UNEASY PATH

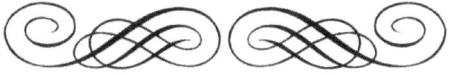

Into the Unknown

Stepping off the gangway onto the dock, an overwhelming sense of awe washed over me.

Even as a soldier who had traveled to many corners of the world, so far, the Philippines were unlike any place I'd ever visited before. A myriad of sensory experiences was unfolding before me, one after the next, each one alien yet just as captivating as the last.

The pier was buzzing with vibrant activity as if nothing at all was amiss around these parts, the boardwalk adorned with people dressed in traditional garments known as the *Barong Tagalog* and *Baro't Saya.* That much, I knew, though not much more.

Intricate embroidery and vibrant designs decorated the people's attire, a testament to the rich heritage and traditions they were known to hold so dear. In the prior weeks, I had done much reading about this place, hence I knew a few of the nuances of the culture and social etiquette, but nothing could have prepared me for being here, seeing what I saw with my own eyes.

Amidst the backdrop of war, an alluring contradiction was already emerging in this place, mingling and merging with the aromatic scents of exotic spices, smoked meats, and fresh fruits.

As I surveyed the scene, this surreal ambiance persisted, only deepening my admiration. The locals seemed so resilient despite the many horrors of war and Japanese occupation, the populace exuding an air of strength. Their clear and tacit commitment to preserving their traditions and cultural identity in the face of such overwhelming adversity left me agog. In the West, it took so little to unsettle and unseat us, to make us panic and to really rattle us.

Here, they clung to their identity as if snuggled inside a lifejacket while bobbing in a roiling sea. Their ship may sink, but they gave me the impression of being far from drowning. War and occupation had no chance of even beginning to erode the values of these people.

With a renewed sense of purpose, my men and I began the arduous task of unloading our supplies from the ships. Just a month earlier, Allied forces had seized the territory of Lingayen Gulf in the Philippines, and a mixture of apprehension and excitement was now coursing through my veins. We had undergone rigorous training for precisely this moment, and finally, the mission was underway. *You've prepared for this. Get the job done,* I told myself.

Yet even as we set about our tasks, the faces of the locals were already creating an indelible impression, turning my former apprehension into ease. Against a backdrop of staged equipment, I observed my men, ready to reclaim what had been rudely snatched away from these resilient men and women. For a moment, I even caught myself wondering if they really needed my help at all, mental strength exuding from their pores. Even the elderly folks sat nonchalantly in the street by the port, taking in everything in silent observation, never flinching. Hypothetically, I imagined that they might even continue to sit there as bombs rained down, stoic and unflinching, before going to pull in their fishing nets in a show of *business as usual.*

This kind of attitude could not be taught to the likes of us. It flowed in their veins.

Our orders were part of a broader mission to liberate the Philippines from Japanese occupation, establishing a base for further operations in the Pacific theater of World War II.

For three years, the Japanese had been subjecting the Philippines to a cruel and disrespectful occupation, exploiting the country's resources, enslaving its people, and inflicting unimaginable suffering without bounds. Now, our purpose was clear: we were here to fight for justice and freedom, and for the right of the Filipino people to live without oppression or fear.

The task ahead was daunting, but we would neither bend nor yield, even less so now we had set eyes on the Filipinos.

Outside a weathered and towering building, I stood, my broad shoulders squared and my military insignia gleaming under a searing sun. Taking a deep breath to steady my nerves, I awaited the arrival of my men. Running a callused hand over the stubble on my chin, apprehension lingered. Years of service in the Army had taught me that each new mission carried its own challenges and potential dangers, and it was when we were new that the greatest dangers lurked.

Approaching me with an expression of surprise, a figure drew nearer; it was Corporal David Chen. It had been years since our paths had crossed, yet seeing him again felt like stepping back in time. David walked up to me; his eyes filled with an equal measure of astonishment.

He thrust out his hand. "Sergeant George Grey? I can't believe it's you!"

A smile played upon my lips as I extended a firm hand to shake his, savoring the familiarity of the moment. "Chen, it's so good to see you," I replied, taking in the sight of his lean, muscular frame that had not changed a bit. He never seemed to grow any older, and I knew the same could not be said for me. "You look good," I added, appreciating his sharp features still carrying the echoes of shared experiences long past. He nodded and grinned broadly, stark white teeth glinting in the sunlight, a testament to a flawlessly heathy diet far more wholesome than my own.

"You too, man," he responded, nodding toward my muscular build and the piercing green eyes that had seen much in my time in the service. His keen attention to detail was evident as he continued, "I see you've kept up with your physical training. That skin fade looks sharp, and the scar above your lip adds to the 'tough guy' look."

A chuckle escaped me at his observation. David always did have the sharpest eye.

"You haven't changed a bit either," I replied, examining him in turn. "Your eyes still hold that piercing gaze, and I'm sure your shooting skills are as keen as ever. Plus, I have to don my sunglasses every time you smile."

He nodded, laughing. Chen was a man of relatively few words when it came to taking compliments; he would merely grin his way through them all.

"Remember that time back at training camp in Wolters, David?" I continued. "Those were some days, huh?" I asked, feeling a rush of nostalgia.

David chuckled softly, his laughter showing an affectionate reminiscence. "Oh, how could I forget? It feels like yesterday we were just fresh-faced recruits, eager and full of excitement. And those damn uniform inspections!" he added, shaking his head playfully.

I nodded, a grin forming as I recalled those moments when we'd fuss over every detail of our uniforms, making sure each crease resembled the edge of a razor blade.

"You had such a knack for land navigation. I knew I could always rely on you to lead the way," he said.

I nodded appreciatively, eyes glinting with a touch of pride. "And you, my friend, were undoubtedly the best shot in our class. I mean, you could hit a bullseye from a mile away,"

"Only because you taught me how to steady my aim," he flattered me.

"Ah, those competitions were something else," I reminisced. "We pushed each other to be better every time, didn't we?"

As we exchanged fond memories of the camaraderie we had shared during training, I couldn't help but feel grateful for the bond we had also built. Those had been some good times indeed, and I cherished each moment we'd spent together, both in training and on the battlefield.

Glancing down at my wristwatch, I noticed that our new platoon captain's arrival was imminent. "Time to make some new memories, Chen. I'll see you inside."

"Soldiers, gather inside and await the arrival of our new captain!" I called out, projecting my voice across the courtyard. As I watched the troops file into the building, a tinge of apprehension crept up. Rumors had circulated within the division, hinting at a tough and demanding leader, one with a formidable reputation.

"He's not someone you argue with," said one.

"Doesn't suffer fools," voiced another.

Well, none of us would like to suffer fools but I thought I knew what the soldier meant.

The old wooden door loomed above me, creaking softly in the gentle breeze. I had given countless orders like this before, each one reminding me of the battles fought and the lives risked. But as I stood there, waiting for our new captain and his orders, a sense of uncertainty staked a claim to me, making me wonder what challenges lay ahead.

Standing at attention with forty other soldiers behind me, I observed Captain Nicholas Monroe stride into the building, a stack of papers in his hand, his expression slightly flustered as if he felt he had arrived late and shown himself up. Regardless, silence enveloped the room as he entered.

"Good afternoon, men. At ease, soldiers," he announced, scanning the faces before him.

Stepping forward and breaking the silence, I spoke up. "Men, listen up! We have some important news regarding our mission."

Captain Monroe cleared his throat, acknowledging me with a nod before proceeding to explain the details of our next mission. "We have been ordered to march to Balete Pass through the northern mountains in two weeks. We'll be traveling at night and will need enough water, food, and ammunition to last. Be prepared for anything, as the terrain won't be easy."

One of the soldiers seized the opportunity to voice his concerns. "Sir, permission to speak?"

"Granted, soldier. Speak up," the captain responded.

"Sir, while we understand the importance of this mission and are ready to go above and beyond, marching through an unknown route in this mountainous region at night presents significant challenges. Can you provide more information about the terrain and risks involved?"

"Private, I understand your concerns, but time is not on our side. We need to move quickly, but I assure you, it's an entirely feasible operation," the captain replied dismissively, without providing further explanation. He shrugged off the inquirer's words without a thought.

Uneasy glances were observable among the men. It was not long before another soldier stepped forward, echoing the concerns. "Sir, it's essential that we are prepared for any unforeseen circumstances we may encounter. The mountainous terrain in the—"

Needless to say, he was cut short.

"As I said, we are well-prepared already, soldier," the captain replied, brushing off the concerns in the same brusque fashion with which he had dismissed the first man's worries.

Sensing the need to gain clarity for the platoon, I stepped forward. "Captain, if I may ask, what should be our priority during this mission, and how soon should we expect any further orders?"

The captain paused, deep in thought, before responding. "Sergeant, our priority should be to keep moving, minimizing wasted time, as we're already against the clock. Give it your best, ensure everyone's safety, and accomplish the mission's objective. As for further orders, we'll be updated soon."

As the captain had yet again failed to address our worries, it became apparent that his focus lay primarily on getting us in and out of the mission within the designated timeline, rather than prioritizing the safety of the platoon. It would be akin to trying to run a marathon in someone else's outsized shoes. But would this captain ever listen to anything but his own voice? It seemed not.

And was there a single thing I could do to protest and elicit a better response?

Again, definitively, no.

At that moment, I couldn't help but think that the rumors circulating about him were true. But as a seasoned soldier, I understood the significance of setting a positive example for my men. My loyalty lay with the Army and the soldiers under my command, so I responded with proper customs and courtesies, determined to maintain good order and discipline.

"Yes, sir, I understand," I replied. My role was to carry out his orders to the best of my ability and ensure the safe return of my men. Anything beyond that, I could not press him for.

Captain Monroe's words resonated with ferocity as he addressed us, his eyes locked on the target. "Men, we have a mission to complete. We've been ordered to march to Balete Pass, and I won't settle for anything less than victory. General MacArthur wants the Philippines, and it's our duty to deliver these lands to him."

He continued in like manner, providing details of the route we would take and the risks that would be involved. As I listened, I felt troubled; if I wasn't grievously mistaken, something in Captain Monroe's voice was again suggesting that he was more focused on his legacy than our safety. Maybe it was his choice of words or his blatant ignorance and habitual disregard of the worries of the soldiers in the platoon, but either way, his attitude was making the back of my neck bristle already. I felt sure that my face must be looking blotched and reddened by now, showing that my blood pressure was soaring higher than I would have liked.

Refusing to let my thoughts get sidetracked, I eyed the captain anew, bringing my full attention back to the room in which he was still talking to a rapt, though plainly uneasy, audience.

"We'll show the enemy what the U.S. Army is made of," Captain Monroe declared, his voice filled with intensity and more than a hint of narcissism. I could not help imagining him at home with his family—that was assuming he had a wife, which he most likely did.

Did he rule over her too, riding roughshod over her input? Was she permitted to hold views of her own? Was he also one of those insisting *children must be seen and not heard?* Probably.

All irrelevant thoughts, of course, but my mind defiantly transported me to them anyway.

And as his words echoed again through the room, I glanced around, wondering if my fellow soldiers shared my concerns. It was difficult to tell; everyone looked fractious and stressed, but an expression of harried concentration wasn't unusual during any new mission briefing.

Examining Captain Monroe closely, I couldn't help but notice that he defied my prior expectations of his stature. He was relatively short, with a slender frame that made him appear almost delicate. His thinning hair was disheveled, framing a face adorned with unremarkable, small eyes and devoid of any visible scars.

Despite his unassuming appearance, however, he exuded a quiet confidence that spoke of an unwillingness to concede on any point, no matter how small.

With a dismissive wave, Captain Monroe concluded the briefing, and a sigh of relief escaped me as he departed. The room now buzzed with the discontent of the men as they voiced their frustrations and apprehensions about the forthcoming mission.

Many of us shared the same doubts and were interested in determining how best to ensure our safety. As we finally dispersed from the room, I made a mental note to discuss these issues with my fellow soldiers, working together to ensure we remained both prepared and safe during the mission ahead. But it would be easier said than done in such difficult terrain at night.

"Easy, men. We've faced worse situations before," I interjected, attempting to steady my men's obvious nerves. "Many tasks seem more daunting than they are discovered to be. Success lies in our rigorous planning."

"But Sergeant Grey, what if—" one soldier began, his voice trailing off, fear lingering in his eyes that darted side to side as if whatever he was thinking was just too frightening to voice.

"*What if?* Let me remind you that we are soldiers. We willingly enlisted, fully aware of the risks," I interrupted firmly, projecting a sense of resolve. "We specialize in risk, do we not? And we mitigate the risks in everything we do. Let's not allow our imaginations to get the best of us. There are no *what ifs.*"

I could sense the tension and unease among the men but couldn't allow them to dwell on Captain Monroe's lack of leadership. A bad first impression could undermine our mission, and for now, it was demanding our utmost focus and sharpness. One hint of weakness or nervousness in me, and the men would entirely lose faith in themselves to carry this mission to a successful completion.

"The captain has his orders, just as we do. But that doesn't mean we can't do our part. We'll remain vigilant, keep each other safe, and fulfill our duties. That's what we've always done, and it's what we'll do now," I assured them, my voice brimming with conviction. If only I'd felt inside of me the same certainty that my voice projected, but it came from years of training to allay men's fears and get the job done, no matter what.

Deep down, I dually acknowledged the importance of addressing their valid concerns. However, at that moment, my primary objective was to instill calm and maintain their focus. We had a mission to accomplish, one that lay within our reach with my leadership and their collective skills. Thankfully, the mumbling and grumbling among the soldiers subsided, replaced by a renewed determination.

"Men, prepare to march to the mountain with all necessary supplies," I commanded, projecting a clear and authoritative tone, ensuring the soldiers were ready for the challenges awaiting us all.

Corporal Chen cleared his throat and stepped forward, his sharp features reflecting his intensified focus on our goal. "You're right, Sergeant. We've endured worse. But that doesn't mean we can let our guard down. We need to be cautious and smart if we hope to make it through this alive."

"That's the spirit, Chen." I nodded approvingly. "And Richardson, remember we're soldiers. We signed up for this and must see it through, even if we might disagree with our commanding officer."

Richardson nodded, his hand thoughtfully stroking his chin. "I understand, Sergeant. But something about the way the captain speaks...it's as if he's more concerned about his own legacy than the safety of his men." He said the precise words that ran through my head.

I could see the concern on Richardson's face but couldn't let him or Chen focus too much on our commanding officer's flaws. We had a critical mission to complete.

"I understand your fears, Private," I responded. "But let's not dwell excessively on just one interaction, all right? We must work together to make this mission successful, regardless of who's leading us. Trust me, I'll have your back, and I know you'll have mine. Now, let's ensure we have everything we need."

As I surveyed the men around me, their frustration continued mounting. Corporal Chen and I were supposed to be overseeing the loading of supplies onto the mules, but here we were, simultaneously boosting morale and maintaining control of the situation. "Listen up, everyone!" I called out, striving to capture their attention. "We must be strategic in loading the mules. We can't simply toss everything on there and hope for the best. Corporal Chen, where do you think we should begin?"

Chen gazed up at me, his head tilting thoughtfully as it always would. "Considering the terrain, we'll be traversing, Sergeant Grey, it would be best to load the heavier supplies toward the front of the mules, ensuring even weight distribution. Additionally, we must balance the load on both sides to prevent any destabilization that could cause the mules to stumble."

I nodded, in agreement with Chen's assessment. "Exactly, but we must also double-check the ropes and secure everything tightly. We can't afford to lose any supplies along the way."

One of the soldiers grumbled, voicing his frustration. "Where's Captain Monroe? Shouldn't he be here assisting us?"

Suppressing my exasperation, I maintained my composure. "Captain Monroe has other duties to attend to. It's our responsibility to transport these supplies to Balete Pass, and that's precisely what we'll do. Any other questions?"

Despite the lingering dissatisfaction, I sensed the soldiers' willingness to listen and learn from Chen and me. "All right then, let's get to work. We're a team, and we need to collaborate to achieve our objectives."

As the men dispersed, each focused on their assigned tasks, I couldn't help but wonder about Captain Monroe's whereabouts too. However, I pushed aside that thought, channeling my energy toward our immediate objectives. The men and I swiftly completed the necessary preparations and were ready to embark on our journey.

***

As we finished, a moment of respite settled in, providing an opportunity for bonding among my men after several hours of arduous work. Private Davis leaned over; his voice filled with curiosity. "Hey, Sarge, while we were sharing stories, we realized we don't know much about you. So, would you like to share some memories with us?"

It clearly was not optional, more a direct request couched as a question. Still, it was well received, and a chuckle escaped my lips, accompanied by a warm feeling in my chest. It never ceased to amaze me how these men, my brothers in arms, extended their concern beyond the battlefield. "Well, Davis, what would you like to know? Ask away. I'm an open book."

He shrugged, settling back on his bedroll. "Anything, Sarge. We want to know more about you."

Pausing briefly, I pondered my reply, selecting my words carefully. It was never easy to talk about myself unless someone posed specific questions; it already felt like being back at school, everyone eyeing me and falling silent as they awaited my two-minute presentation to the "class."

"Well, I grew up on a farm in Texas, you know. My family faced financial struggles, and that's why I joined the Army—to provide support. I never expected to stay this long, but war has a way of reshaping one's path. I'm sure I'm not the only one to say so."

Silence hung there for a moment, their gazes pressing upon me. Finally, one of the soldiers spoke quietly, asking, "Do you still send money home, Sarge?"

Nodding, a surge of pride flushed my cheeks. "Every opportunity I get. It may not be much, but it helps keep the farm going. I owe them that much, you know?"

A murmur of respect rippled through the men, and Davis clapped me on the shoulder. "We're lucky to have you here, Sarge. Your family must be proud of you."

A soft smile formed, the warmth in my chest reigniting. "I hope so, Davis. I truly hope so."

As midday passed, all the men gathered to share stories, laughter, and dreams of the future. Tales of love and longing were told with pride and warmth, each soldier speaking of his cherished woman back home, yearning for the day he could return and marry his beloved. In those moments, we solidified as brothers, and it felt as though they had my back just the same way I had theirs. It was an honor to serve with them and, even more so, to share a piece of my story.

As we prepared to resume our journey, Captain Monroe materialized out of nowhere, catching us off guard. His commanding presence and barking voice unsettled the atmosphere. "What's the meaning of this, Sergeant?" he demanded, his gaze sweeping across the men. Evidently, he did not like to see the men at ease in my presence.

Suppressing my annoyance, I responded evenly, "Sir, we were taking a moment to catch our breath before the march to Balete Pass. The men have completed their tasks and are ready to move out."

Monroe's lips curled into a sneer; his tone filled with condescension. "Resting, Sergeant? This isn't a vacation. No one should be standing around. Get these men moving, now."

Taking a deep breath to maintain composure, I approached him, speaking in a hushed tone meant for his ears alone. "With all due respect, sir, the men have been working tirelessly and deserve a brief respite. We face a long and arduous march ahead, and we must ensure they are in top shape if we are to make it through."

Monroe stepped closer, his voice a low whisper of secrecy as if imparting classified information. "I understand, Sergeant. However, consider appearances. Some higher-ups are growing impatient with our progress, and we all must demonstrate our competence."

I nodded slowly, realizing this was more about perception than reality. "I see what you mean, sir. Maybe we can speed things up without making the men feel rushed. What do you suggest?"

But he did not suggest anything. Instead, Monroe's expression relaxed slightly, and he clapped me on the shoulder. "That's exactly what I was thinking, Sergeant. Now, who has my M1 carbine and pistol?"

I hesitated momentarily, caught off guard by his request as I grabbed his weapons. "Here you go, sir."

He took the weapons in hand, tucking them under his arm. "Thanks, Sergeant. Now let's get moving. I want our best man at the formation front. I'll hold the rear to ensure no one's left behind."

This was a first, I thought. Typically, the Captain and I would continue to lead the formation until we entered a combat zone so everyone could see any signals we gave. Especially with this terrain, we would converse through. "Yes, sir," I said quietly, acquiescing.

"Corporal Chen, you and I will navigate the platoon. Everyone else, gather your belongings and weapons. It's time to head north!" I commanded.

"Yes, Sergeant!" Corporal Chen shouted, rallying the men as they prepared their gear and shouldered their weapons.

I'd been in combat before, but this still felt different, since being a leader in these circumstances was something, I'd never done. A cold fear was creeping up my gut, making me unsure if I was at all ready to lead my platoon into this mission. As I gave orders to my fellow soldiers, I could see the uncertainty in their eyes. Based on my brief encounters with the captain, the burden of leadership pressed down on me even more.

As we ventured forth, I was steeling myself for the worst, mentally preparing for the possibility of taking lives or losing my own, my mind taking me into negative places, thoughts I always refused to let my men's thoughts wander to. Adrenaline was coursing through my veins, heightening my senses as I led my men toward the unknown. Each step drew us closer to the enemy's domain, and with every stride, I became increasingly embroiled in a silent battle against the burgeoning inner fears, relying on discipline, instincts, and training to guide me.

Now, more than ever, I couldn't afford to succumb to these destructive anxieties.

Reminding myself of my extensive training, I knew I possessed the skills necessary to seek cover, navigate hostile terrain, and give life-saving orders. However, taking that first step into the unknown would always be a terrifying experience for anyone. In the back of my mind, echoes of my training instructor's voice resonated, emphasizing the importance of mastering one's fear— an essential trait setting leaders apart from the rest.

Love and Loyalty

Our platoon continued marching toward Balete Pass, the mountains looming closer and closer. The rugged terrain before us grew increasingly challenging, the rocky paths and steep slopes testing both our physical and mental stamina. Though I could sense the unease in my men, it was clear they were a resilient and well-trained bunch who wouldn't falter. They were prepared for this mission, their determination evident in every step they took.

We continued our journey in silence, the crunch of our boots on the rocky ground being the only sound breaking through the stillness. Each one of us was lost in our thoughts, contemplating the uncertainties that lay ahead. Our mission was growing increasingly burdensome, a dreadful weariness beginning to set in as we trudged onward.

But then, as if in response to a collective sigh of relief, I called out, "All right, men! Time to set up camp for the night. Find a suitable spot, and let's get to work."

The men welcomed the prospect of rest with cheers, quickly springing into action. Some set about gathering firewood to light a comforting blaze, while others expertly pitched tents, providing shelter from the elements. The clanging of pots and pans signaled the start of dinner preparations, the aromas soon mingling with the earthy scent of our surroundings.

I took the opportunity to walk around and inspect the campsite, ensuring that everything was orderly and secure, as our safety was paramount.

As Johnson motioned toward the breathtaking view of the mountains, painted in fiery colors by the setting sun, I couldn't help but be captivated by the natural beauty before us. The mountains seemed to glow with an ethereal light, sending long shadows over our campsite. It was a moment of tranquility amidst our tumultuous journey, but I reminded the men to stay vigilant. In these unfamiliar lands, we couldn't afford to let our guard down.

With the camp fully set up, we gathered around the crackling fire, its glow creating an orange tone on our faces. We sat together, sharing our rations, stories, and laughter. In that moment, the camaraderie between us was palpable, a powerful force that would sustain us through the challenging times ahead.

As the night approached, I divided the men, sending half to rest while the others kept watch. I settled into a chair by the fire, taking a moment to savor the peaceful calm surrounding us, listening to the crackling of the flames. The wind had died down, and a sense of serenity enveloped our campsite.

Captain Monroe approached me by the fire, his eyes themselves ablaze with ambition. "Sergeant," he said in a low, urgent tone. "How much longer until we reach the mountains?"

"We're making steady progress, sir," I replied, striving to keep my tone composed. "But we must prioritize safety and steadiness. Rushing could lead to grave mistakes we cannot afford."

"I understand your concern, Sergeant," he replied, his voice hard. "But we can't let caution slow us down either. We have to keep moving forward, no matter what."

I could sense the frustration and nervousness in his voice, the obsession with succeeding no matter the cost. Evidently, his vision for the mission was quite different from mine.

"Captain, I know what you're trying to achieve, and I understand your sense of urgency," I said, my voice firm. "But our top priority has to be the safety of our men. We can't push them to move too quickly or risk losing them."

"I *won't* risk losing them," he said, his voice rising slightly. "But we have to succeed, Sergeant. We have to do whatever it takes to complete the mission. It's no time for hesitancy."

"I agree, Captain, but we must find a balance," I insisted, meeting his eyes with my own. "We can't forget the reason we're here. Families are waiting for us back home, and we must return to them. That has to be our top priority."

Captain Monroe was silent momentarily, an awkward tension building between us. But then he nodded slowly, his face softening a little.

"I know, and I do understand, Sergeant," he said, his voice calmer. "You're right. Our men are our top priority, and I'll ease up on the pressure as long as we get there." I nodded, "We will get there, and we will get back. We all want to hold our children again."

A sense of relief came washing over me, knowing that Captain Monroe had listened to reason—and not just listened, but he had *heard* too. We sat there by the crackling fire, both lost in our thoughts as the men around settled in for the night, their faces bathed in the firelight.

"Hey, Sarge, Captain," Chen said, sitting beside us. "You guys look as though you're having a serious discussion."

"Just talking strategy, Corporal," I said, smiling. "What's going on with you?"

Chen grinned and shook his head. "Nothing much, Sarge. Just enjoying the peace. We rarely get to sit by the fire and relax, as you know."

Captain Monroe chuckled as he stood up, announcing that he would see us early in the morning. "Goodnight, sir," I said, and couldn't help but think that Chen's remark might have convinced him we were moving too slowly.

Chen moved closer to me, expressing his gratitude. "Hey, Sarge," he said. "Thanks for looking out for us."

I laughed and replied, "It's my job, Corporal. But you're most welcome."

Still admiring the breathtaking view of the mountains surrounding us, Chen broke the silence once more. "So, Sarge, tell me what's new with you. What's happened since Europe? Do you have a lady back home?"

I hesitated for a moment, contemplating whether to share my feelings. But I trusted Chen and decided to confide in him about the woman I had been admiring near my farm. "Well, Chen, there's this beautiful woman I have my eye on. But I've never dared to tell her how I feel. Plus, I guess I've just been too preoccupied with my military service."

Chen's eyes lit up with excitement as he encouraged me, "Why not take the leap of faith, Sarge? Who knows what might happen?"

I shrugged, unsure of how to approach the situation. "I don't know, Chen. It's challenging to find the right time, not least when the military keeps sending us to fight wars. Even if she happened to be interested in me, how could a fair and honorable man build a woman's hopes like that, only to dash them again so soon?"

Understanding my dilemma, Chen nodded empathetically. "I feel you, man. It's tough being away from the ones we love. I miss my girl so much. And you're right. You'll find the perfect time to talk to her about how you feel."

His words resonated deeply with me, reminding me of the ache in my heart whenever I thought of the woman I liked. "It is tough," I agreed, my voice laden with emotion. "But yes, there'll come a suitable time."

Chen's optimistic spirit shone through as he encouraged us both to focus on our mission and ensure a safe return to our loved ones. "We have each other here," he said. "And with that, we'll return to our families safe and sound."

I sat there, basking in the warmth of the campfire and the camaraderie with Chen. As he spoke about his amazing girlfriend and his plans to propose, I couldn't help but feel affected by all this. On the one hand, I was genuinely happy for him, knowing how deeply he cared for her and the excitement he felt about their future together. On the other hand, I couldn't ignore the pang of jealousy tugging at my heartstrings. While Chen's love life seemed so well-organized, I was still grappling with my feelings for the woman who had captured my thoughts, unsure of how to express them even if the opportunity did happen to come along sometime in the future.

Chen's infectious enthusiasm and hope that I might find my own happiness gave me a glimmer of encouragement. Perhaps someday, I would have the courage to open my heart and share my feelings with this lady. She had been captivating my thoughts for years.

As he bade me good night and walked away, I found myself alone by the campfire, lost in my thoughts again. I reached into my pocket and pulled out a letter I had been carrying for far too long. It was one I had written in secret, pouring my heart and soul onto the pages. No one knew about it, and it was a risk to put my feelings into words, but something about her urged me to take this chance. Her warm smile and kind eyes had always made me feel at home, even amidst the chaos of war. She was the anchor in my life, the missing piece that would complete me. Yet fear and doubt held me back, making me hesitate with every attempt to express myself.

The passing years had done nothing to diminish my affection for her, but the demands of military service had kept me from finding the right moment to reveal my feelings. Now, surrounded by the tranquility of the night, the stars shining above, and listening to the gentle crackling of the fire, I knew deep within that this was the opportune moment to unburden my heart.

I took a deep breath and started writing, letting the words flow onto the pages without inhibition. Every emotion, every longing, and every hope spilled onto that letter in a cathartic release, and with each word, the weight on my chest lifted more.

As I finished the handwritten missive, this was a pivotal moment that could change everything. The mystery and suspense surrounding my sentiments for her had kept this letter hidden for too long, but now it was time to take that leap of faith of which Chen had spoken so well.

I carefully folded the paper and secured it back in my pocket, knowing that soon, it would find its way to her, and with it, a piece of my heart would go too. I couldn't predict her reaction or the outcome, but the mere act of finally expressing myself brought a sense of peace and courage.

The first light of dawn bathed the Philippine mountains in a misty haze as our platoon stirred awake, ready to continue our arduous journey. The dense jungle around us was already alive with the sounds of nature, but we couldn't afford to let our guard down. We had ventured deep into enemy territory, every rustle of leaves setting our hearts pounding with paranoia.

As we marched on relentlessly, the treacherous jungle terrain challenged us at every step. Slippery mud and thick underbrush threatened to trip us up at every turn, and the fear of a mistimed step leading to a dangerous fall kept us alert. Despite it all, we knew we had to push forward at a steady and unrelenting pace; our orders were clear, and there was no turning back.

Captain Monroe's determination remained evident in his eyes as he led the way. However, I couldn't shake my unease, still fearing that his immoveable approach might lead us into unnecessary danger sooner or later. The men's silent steps confirmed they felt it too.

Suddenly, Corporal Chen's voice crackled over the radio, sending a chill down my spine. "Sergeant, you won't believe this. I've spotted Japanese forces up ahead." I quickly signaled the platoon to get into battle positions, tension mounting, preparing for a confrontation.

The attack came swiftly, bullets raining down on us as explosions juddered the ground. Amidst the unwelcome melee, I tried to maintain composure and coordinate the platoon's efforts. My heart pounded in my chest, but I had to stay focused to lead our men to safety.

I attempted to communicate with Captain Monroe through the radio, but the dense jungle was interfering with our signals, making it challenging to coordinate effectively. If only he had been closer to me, we could have avoided this communication barrier. Despite the static, I managed to hear the captain's voice, though it was garbled and barely comprehensible.

"Sergeant, what's the situation?" Monroe shouted over the gunfire.

"It's not looking good, Captain!" I yelled back. "We need to disperse into smaller groups to flank them!" My concern for the safety of our men was mounting, and I urgently tried to convince him that overwhelming the enemy wasn't the best approach.

However, Monroe remained stubborn, refusing to heed my warning yet again. "We need to handle this on our own, with force!" he insisted.

The situation grew increasingly dire as the battle pressed on. Our men were falling, some severely wounded, and the enemy was showing no signs of relenting. My heart sank with each casualty, frustration mounting as I saw the consequences of not adapting our strategy.

If we didn't disperse, we would continue to lose men, the mission ending in certain disaster. I tried again to convince the captain, but my pleas fell on deaf ears, or the signal was lost in the jungle terrain. I acted quickly, signaling to the men to disperse. We had the advantage of numbers, as there were maybe only twenty to thirty Japanese soldiers.

My heart still would not settle as my platoon engaged the enemy deep within the dense Philippine jungle. Their guerrilla fighters had the advantage of knowing the terrain and holding the element of surprise. It was tense as we formed a c-shape, creeping ever closer.

As we approached, Corporal Chen flanked the enemy position while the rest took cover behind the trees and rocks surrounding us. Gunfire echoed through the jungle, and we opened fire, trying to take the enemy by maneuver. Several bullets came my way as I lay flat behind a tall tree with expansive roots coming out of its vast trunk. We were in the thick of things now. The enemy was well-prepared, forcing us to take cover behind anything we could find. Every step felt like a potential trap, and I had to make split-second decisions to keep my men from harm.

But as we engaged the enemy, our radio crackled to life, Captain Monroe's voice commanding us to regroup. It was a moment of confusion and panic as we struggled to move to safety.

But suddenly, the orders were reversed, and we were told to hold our position. A moment of intense disarray followed as my platoon scrambled to regroup and continue the fight. I looked back to see where the captain was, hoping to better understand the change of direction, eventually spotting his captain's bars shining from his helmet. He was about ten feet away from me, hiding behind several rocks and a natural hill that covered him well, minus his head. I shouted, "Cover me!" as the men did just that so I could run back and check on the captain.

I reached the captain's location as bullets and screams resounded.

Soon, I discovered Captain Monroe crouched behind a dense bush a few feet from the platoon's position. "Captain, everything okay? We've got to scatter with the close quarters and lack of cover. We need to move quickly, sir," I said, panting. "The enemy's closing in, and we're pinned down."

He looked at me, his face twisted with anxiety. "I'm struggling, Sergeant," he admitted unexpectedly, his voice shaking. "I'm struggling to decide how we get out of this."

His words hit me hard. In our short time working side by side, the captain had seemed very determined and ambitious, but now,

I saw a man already struggling to cope with the stress of combat. I placed a hand on his shoulder, trying to convey my support.

"Listen, sir," I said. "We have to figure this out and fast."

He looked at me, his eyes full of emotion. "You're right, Sergeant," he said, his voice more certain. "We need unity of direction."

We both knew what needed to be done. We needed to give our men clear directives, stay focused, and work together if we were to make it out alive.

As we began to move forward, the Japanese guerrilla fighters opened fire. We were pinned down, and things were looking dire. But we couldn't give up. "Keep moving, men!" I shouted, trying to keep their spirits up. "We can do this! Stay low and keep firing!"

Out of nowhere, there appeared in my right eye a Japanese soldier, charging at me with a long knife gripped in his right hand. Our bodies collided quickly as we fell to the ground, and his knife dropped about three feet away. He was fierce, his strength considerable as we exchanged blows. He had been trained well, and I was outmatched but refused to give up, salty sweat pouring down my face as we grappled with each other.

We were so close that I could smell the stench of hunger on his breath. I tried to stay composed, but the jarring sound of gunfire in the distance was rendering me increasingly anxious.

Just when I thought it was over, another voice came. "Sergeant, look out!" This was Captain Monroe, now returned to his senses. He picked up the knife and charged the Japanese soldier, plunging the blade deep into his chest.

As the Japanese fighter fell to the ground, lifeless, I looked up at the captain with a sense of respect. But as I searched to meet his eyes, only shock and horror adorned his face. The situation's intensity had taken its toll on him, and he was struggling to hold on. I put my hand on his shoulder, reassuring him yet again. "It's okay, Captain," I said, keeping him calm. "We're still here and will make it out of this together. Calm your fears, sir."

It dawned on me that the captain had never been in combat before.

We both took a moment to catch our breath before moving on. The battle raged around us, and we still had a mission to complete. We couldn't let the loss of our fallen comrades, or the intensity of the combat slow us. As we continued fighting through the jungle, the captain was regaining confidence, seemingly following my own lead. He took charge too, giving clear directions to the men and making quick decisions. After several hours, the sounds of bullets and screams were over. We had won the battle, emerging as victors with only a few casualties and wounded.

Exhausted and under his breath, the captain said, "Sergeant Grey, have five men escort our casualties and wounded back to headquarters. The rest of us here will set up camp and press on early tomorrow."

"Yes, sir; all right, men. You heard the captain. Let's start setting up camp."

I made my way over to pay my respects to our fallen men, the worst part of the war. I had known these young men and all their dreams, knowing they had sacrificed everything to be here. Now, they were gone due to their dedication. Their mothers would soon receive the bitter news from which they would never recover, news that would destroy even more lives. Placing my hands on each one, I said a short prayer, praying that the souls of our fallen men would find peace forever, that their sacrifice wouldn't have been for nothing.

Perhaps shutting my mind to everything else, the only things I heard that night were the exotic animals and the wind blowing through the trees.

***

The next two days luckily emerged to be far less eventful, and soon, we received word that our men had returned to headquarters safely.

I adjusted my rucksack and sucked in a deep breath as my platoon emerged into the mountain range from the dense jungle terrain. Two long days of travel through the jungle had taken their toll on us, but seeing the mountains gave us a renewed sense of purpose. We were only about three days away from Balete Pass by now, our final destination.

Captain Monroe approached me, Corporal Chen also heading over to join us. "Sergeant Grey, we'll have aerial support this time," Monroe said. "Intel confirms that the enemy has dug in and will be in close-quarters combat."

I nodded, my mind racing with the implications of aerial support. This operation had not been in the works for long, and the promise of aerial support made it seem too good to be true. Close-quarters combat wouldn't be easy, but we were ready for this challenge. Corporal Chen snickered beside me. "Oh yeah, a little birdie's gonna come swoop in and save us all," he said.

I shot a quick scowl his way before turning back to the captain.

"Sir, I've a good feeling about this operation. We've trained extensively for this type of combat, and with aerial support, we'll have the upper hand."

Captain Monroe nodded. "We don't know what the enemy has up their sleeve."

"Oh, come on, sir. We got this in the bag," joked Corporal Chen.

I quickly interjected, "Don't underestimate the enemy. They've been preparing for this too."

"That's right," offered Monroe, nodding. "We need to stay cautious and vigilant. If we let our guard down, that's when they'll pounce again. Corporal Chen, think before you speak."

We continued our march, keeping the looming battle ahead as our motivation. The chatter among the platoon died down as we all reflected on what was to come.

Eventually, Captain Monroe pulled me aside as we set up camp for the night. "Sergeant Grey, I wanted to review our strategy with you."

I nodded, my hearing at attention, glad he was including me in the planning and strategy; I possessed years of experience of doing this and didn't want to lose any more men.

Captain Monroe continued, "The enemy has dug in, and we'll go in close quarters. We'll need to move quickly and be strategic with our movements. I want you to have your squad in charge of taking out any snipers in the area and any mortar positions."

I nodded, my mind racing with the possibilities. Close-quarters combat was always intense, and now, we had a specific target to go after. I quickly ran the plan through my head, and everything seemed feasible. But then again, you never knew what would happen in battle.

Corporal Chen wandered over, asking, "What's the plan, boss?"

I quickly filled him in, telling him his squad would remove any artillery positions. He nodded, and I could see the fire in his eyes, confirming he was itching for battle.

We set up watches with rotating shifts, and I took the first. Scanning the surroundings for any signs of the enemy, the faint chug of a helicopter rose in the distance. A smile spread, realizing the extent of the operation in which we were involved: aerial support.

The rest of the night passed uneventfully, and as the first light broke the next morning, we got up early to start on the next leg of our journey. The mountains posed a welcome change from the sweltering jungle terrain, but the ascent was steep and grueling. As we continued, the tension was both palpable and mounting. We were closing in on Balete Pass by now, and the possibility of engaging in combat was increasing with every step. The thought of close-quarters combat was sending a shiver down my spine, but I had to remain grounded and focused.

We reached the top of the mountain, and I took a moment to look at the views. The vast expanse of the landscape was breathtaking, a testament to the sheer natural beauty of this country. My musings were interrupted by the captain. "All right, Sergeant. We need to get moving."

We quickly made our way down the mountainside, my heart rate accelerating anew as I pondered on what was to come. We were getting much closer to Balete Pass now, the wariness showing in my platoon's eyes.

As we stopped for a brief respite, Captain Monroe approached. "Sergeant, we just received intel that the enemy has moved most of their reinforcements to Balete Pass," he said. "Our recon teams have reported heavy artillery and anti-aircraft placements."

I nodded, my mind racing with the implications. We would face heavy resistance and had no idea what kind of weaponry they might have at their disposal. We would need to stay cautious and vigilant if we wanted to make it out of this alive.

The captain continued, "We must be aggressive with our movements. We can't allow them to get too comfortable. That's when they'll make their move."

I nodded, my mind busy, already formulating a plan.

This is it. We're about to engage in close quarters combat with a well-armed and prepared enemy, I told myself. *But I'm ready for it.*

We'd been preparing for this for months; I wasn't going to let all that training go to waste.

A Battle in the Mountains

My platoon and I trekked through the mountainous terrain for days, getting closer to Balete Pass, our pulses rising and our anxieties alongside. Now, just three days away from our objective, the challenge was still looming in our minds, some of us conceding to ourselves that it seemed insurmountable. But I dared not allow myself to think it since reclaiming this strategic location would be vital for the success of our entire operation. War, and all the terror that it would bring, was looming over us all, the enemy's presence lurking in a constant dark shadow of foreboding.

As we trudged through the rugged terrain, our gear burdened us, the scorching heat sapping our strength. The dust-filled roads with their potholes seemed endless, exhaustion gnawing away at our spirits. Yet, determination fueling our steps, we had to press on.

A collective apprehension mounted under the increasing physical and mental strain. Discipline was our lifeline, for losing control could spell disaster. We knew the enemy was watching us by now, tracking our every step, anticipating each move, and preparing to strike.

With each passing step, the chaos of the war was becoming ever more evident, the smell of smoke and gunpowder growing stronger. We grew increasingly silent in our talk and even our breaths, each man pensive and filled with tough questions to which we possessed no answers yet. The many *what ifs* I had earlier banned could still be felt, though no one gave a voice to them.

Ahead of us lay a daunting task that would mean the difference between life and death. But we had no time to think, no time to hesitate.

Just beyond the horizon, the enemy was lurking, forcing us to summon courage and ready our weapons for an impending battle. The stakes were crystal clear; it was a case of *fight or perish.*

Our feelings became a reality when Corporal Chen's frantic shout of "Cover!" echoed in the breeze. The enemy was here, and what's more, they were ready for battle. The sound of gunfire crackled in the atmosphere as we quickly dropped to the ground, seeking shelter behind any nearby rocks we could find.

Captain Monroe frantically pulled out his radio to call for backup, but the gadget remained silent. We were outnumbered and outgunned, and even worse, we were on our own.

Fear and anxiety swept through the platoon as we huddled behind cover, unsure from which direction the enemy was firing on us as yet. The tension was thick as we waited for the enemy soldiers to reveal their next move. Suddenly, they emerged from concealed positions, armed to the teeth and ready for us. Our hearts were pounding, but we refused to back down.

With war's harsh symphony deafening our ears, I signaled my squad to advance, seeking cover as we closed in on the enemy. The clash was intense, a blur of close-quarters combat, hand-to-hand struggles, and grenade explosions. There came an overwhelming acrid smell of cordite as we fought on, buoyed by adrenaline and flanked by an overwhelming fear of death.

I noticed Captain Monroe taking cover behind a nearby tree and quickly joined him, seeking guidance. The desperation in his eyes appeared almost tangible, a sign that he knew we were facing overwhelming odds right now and needed a plan to turn the tide. Combat had its effect on all of us, even our valiant leader. I had to get him back in the fight.

"Captain, we have to flush them out," I shouted above the din. "Use the rocket launchers and grenades to scatter them!" He seemed momentarily frozen as if far too overwhelmed by it all, but I grabbed his arm, urging him, "Captain, we need you in this fight!"

Sweat was dripping down my forehead as we took up position huddling behind the rocks, our senses heightened to the extreme. But nothing could have prepared us for what happened next.

A sudden thud sounded, our heads snapping up, scanning for its source. Then, we saw it, a small black object hurtling toward us. A grenade.

Time seemed to slow as my mind raced through possibilities. Running felt futile, and there was no escape. Captain Monroe's voice echoed but was difficult to make out amid the chaos. We all dove for cover, bracing for the impact.

The grenade landed perilously close to the captain before exploding with a deafening boom, a blinding flash engulfing the terrain all around, the ground quaking beneath us. For a moment, the world was chaos, our senses overwhelmed by the blast.

As the smoke cleared, my heart sank. Captain Monroe was lying on the ground on his back, wounded and bleeding. The smell of burnt metal and gunpowder overpowered my sense of smell as I rushed to his side. His eyes were open but fading, an immense panic surging within me. "Medic!"

Combat medics hurried over, assessing his wounds with urgency. Blood was pooling on the rocky ground as they worked quickly to tend to him; there was no doubt he was bleeding out, every second seeing his life force gushing free, each pump of his heart releasing vital redness that was already stealing all the light from his eyes.

"He's lost a lot of blood," one medic murmured, his voice tense.

"But his vitals are stable," the other medic replied unbelievably. My thought was, *how can that be? He's lost way too much blood already, surely.* But sure enough, the medic was pointing to the captain's pulse. My mind was racing, searching for the best course of action. I looked down at him, terrible pain contorting his face. His uniform had been torn apart, revealing the severity of his injuries. Miraculously, he had survived, but his condition remained precarious.

"We need to get him to a field hospital as soon as possible," I declared resolutely. "But how do we do it?"

The medics exchanged a glance, and one of them spoke up. "We need to get out of the mountains and radio for support," he suggested. "His wounds are severe, and we can't treat him properly here. Look at this place. It's—"

"We can transport him back for surgery," the other medic finished, nodding in agreement.

I assessed the situation, considering the risks and possibilities before nodding in consent. "All right," I said. "Move quickly and stay safe."

Their plan was set in motion. The platoon provided cover as the medics carefully and urgently lifted the captain to his feet. He looked at me, breaking his silence. "Lead these men as you have," he said, his voice strained, breathy.

"Yes, sir. See you when this is over," I replied, determined to keep his confidence in my leadership. "You'll be all right, sir."

The medics exchanged a knowing look, displaying that they had done everything in their power to ensure his survival. "He's going to make it," one medic said quietly, a note of honesty and relief in his voice. "I'm sure of it. At least I'd like to think so."

I'd like to think so was hardly the vote of certainty I thought he had just delivered.

The other nodded firmly, his resolve also firm. "Yes," he said too. "He's going to make it. We won't let him down."

But there was something I felt they failed to comprehend. It was that whether a man lived or died had little to do with being "let down" or being supported by his brothers in arms. We never did let any man down, but still, many passed into the afterlife regardless—if there even was such a thing.

As the battle raged on, we fought with all our might, determined not to back down. The enemy soldiers pressed harder, pushing us into close-quarters combat. But we remained steadfast, using every tactic we could to outmaneuver them. We were fighting with unity and skill, taking down enemy soldiers one by one until none was left standing.

When the dust finally settled and the gunfire ceased, I surveyed the aftermath. Our platoon had taken its fair share of hits, wounded soldiers lying scattered about. I made sure to check on each one, offering encouragement and ensuring they received medical attention.

I approached Corporal Chen, his expression grim as he took in the grievous sight.

"What's the situation, Corporal?" I asked, knowing the weight of his own unspoken question that burned in his eyes.

He looked up at me, his lips a thin line. He did not answer. "What are we going to do now?" he said, gesturing at the wounded soldiers being tended to. He trailed off, not needing to say any more. I knew what he was implying. The captain was badly wounded, and it wasn't looking good.

But I couldn't allow myself to get distracted by that thought. We needed to keep moving, keep pushing forward toward our objective.

The moment overwhelmed me as I addressed the men, trying to maintain composure despite the turmoil inside my brain. It felt as though I had been fitted out with a suit ten times too stiff and large for my small frame, and now I had been instructed to walk too many miles in it.

"Captain Monroe is being taken care of by the medics," I announced, my voice steady and resolute. "He's on his way to seek support for his injuries."

The soldiers looked at me, concern etched on their demeanors. "What about us, Sergeant?" one of them asked, voicing the men's collective worry. "Are we supposed to continue toward Balete Pass without the captain?"

The question hit me hard. Captain Monroe might have had his flaws, but he had still been our leader, and we'd been relying on his guidance. Now, I was left with the responsibility of leading the platoon, a task I had never faced before. Doubt set in afresh, gnawing at the edges of my mind, but I had to push it aside.

"We keep moving forward," I said firmly, squaring my shoulders. "We can't afford to halt our progress now, not when our objective is within reach. We all know what the objective is, and nothing has changed. We do as our Captain said."

The men exchanged glances, absorbing my words, a sense of unity settling in among us. I could see the eagerness in their eyes, happy and at peace with my certain answer.

It was all they needed, for now anyway. But it was dually clear they were counting on me to lead them, and I couldn't let them down.

Reaching for Corporal Chen's radio, I tried to contact higher headquarters for support, hoping for backup or at least some guidance. But to my dismay, all my attempts to establish communication met with silence. Our isolation had suddenly become apparent, and a surge of worry was coursing through me. We were cut off from any support, stranded without reinforcements.

The reality of our situation was threatening to overwhelm me, but I just couldn't afford to panic. There was no room for that in this life, and every man knew it, though some of us coped better than others.

Amidst the radio's static, a faint crackle gave a glimmer of hope. Leaning in, I strained to hear the voice that buzzed and crackled its way through the chaos. "CHARLIE-SEVEN," the voice said, finally breaking through the interference. "This is VICTOR."

Relief washed over me; we were finally in contact with higher headquarters, so at least we weren't completely alone now. My pulse was beginning to settle back into a more regular, acceptable rhythm, something that had been eluding me for some time under the strain.

But the voice on the other end paused, my heart sinking as it continued, "Sergeant Grey, we've received word of Captain Monroe's injuries. We're sending support to recover him."

Silence fell over us, broken only by the hiss of the radio's interminable static.

But then something strange happened again, the voice setting off speaking anew, but this time, with a far greater message to impart. "Sergeant Grey," the voice said. "You're the senior man on the ground. You have been battlefield promoted to Second Lieutenant."

I stare at the radio in disbelief, barely able to process what was happening. But then I snapped back to reality. I was the leader now, the fate of these men resting on my shoulders. I resolved in that moment to do the best job I could, for the men and for Captain Monroe.

"Roger that VICTOR, CHARLIE-SEVEN will continue to objective, Bravo. Out."

As a newly commissioned platoon commander, I brought Corporal Chen and key team members together to discuss our orders and objectives for moving forward in Balete Pass. The situation was critical, and the stakes high. This was a make-or-break moment for our platoon, and I wanted to ensure a clear plan of attack.

"All right, gentlemen, here's what we know," I began. "We're moving into Balete Pass to secure the enemy's supply lines. Our mission is to cut off their supplies and weaken their position. We've got to move fast and take control of the Pass as quickly as possible."

"What kind of resistance can we expect, sir?" one of the men asked.

"Intelligence reports suggest heavy resistance," I replied. "The enemy is dug deep and has all the advantages."

"Sounds like a hell of a fight," Corporal Chen said.

"It will be," I agreed. "But we've a job to do, and we can't let that intimidate us."

The room fell silent for a moment as we all considered the dangers of the situation. Morale was critical, and I needed to inspire confidence in my men.

"All right let's talk strategy," I said, turning to the group. "What do you all think is the best way to secure our objective?"

Sergeant Miller immediately spoke up. "Sir, it's best if we hit the enemy with a flanking maneuver. If we come down on them from the sides, we can divide their forces and take them by surprise."

"That's a good idea," I said, nodding. "What about support and fire suppression?"

Several men jumped in. "We can use our mortar teams to lay heavy fire on the enemy positions. That should keep them pinned down while we await the attack."

I listened to their ideas, taking note of their experience and expertise.

I had more experience than most of my men combined but wanted to hear their ideas. If this were solely my plan, it would end in defeat. My men had different experiences in combat than I did, and I needed their insight to succeed.

"Okay, so we've got a plan for the attack," I said, looking around the room. "But what about our follow-up strategy? Once we secure the Pass, what's next?"

Corporal Chen offered his contribution, strong as always. "We need to establish a strong perimeter around the Pass and start to fortify our position. That'll make it harder for the enemy to retake the Pass once we're gone."

"That's a good idea," I said. "We should also make sure we're using our engineers to clear the area of any traps or mines left behind by the enemy."

Corporal Chen added his further thoughts. "What about communication, sir? We must ensure we can stay in contact with our higher-ups and support teams."

"You're right," I said, impressed by his insight. "We'll need to set up communication lines as soon as possible. And we must be prepared to adjust our strategy as the situation evolves."

The area fell silent for a moment as we all considered our plan. It was risky, offering no guarantee of success. But my men were ready for the challenge, and we could achieve our objective if we worked together.

"All right, everyone," I said, rising to my feet. "Let's get to work."

Purpose filled our hearts until the static sounded afresh, a radio call coming through from our higher headquarters, VICTOR. My heart was racing as I took it, knowing this could change everything. "CHARLIE-SEVEN, this is VICTOR. We've just received intel that there are five hundred Filipino soldiers located two miles east of your position. They're planning to attack tomorrow, and we need you to move in and help secure the area."

My mind raced, listening to the news; it was great as now, my men could focus on less ground.

"Understood, VICTOR," I replied. "What's our next move?"

"We've secured their radio frequency for you," VICTOR said. "You'll need to link up with their commanding officer and coordinate your plan of attack. We'll send support once we've got the situation under control."

I took a deep breath, knowing this was critical for our platoon. We had to be agile and flexible, quickly adjusting our strategy to accommodate this new threat.

"All right, everyone," I said, turning to my men. "Looks like there are now five hundred more reasons to take Balete Pass. In other words, five hundred Filipino soldiers are ready to reclaim their land alongside us."

With a quick inhale, I braced myself, firmly wedging my hand onto the frequency dial of our radio. I gripped the push-to-talk button tightly, channeling my nerves, making contact with their commander on the other end.

"This is CHARLIE-SEVEN, radio check," I said, speaking into the radio.

There was a brief pause before the commander spoke up. "This is Commander Alvarez." The crackling static in my ear was relentless, muddying Commander Alvarez's response. I braced myself, holding onto the cumbersome radio equipment tightly, and I couldn't help but feel a pang of frustration. We were on a mission requiring clear communication, and the interference was causing me to miss critical information. Why must this happen right now?

"Loud and clear, CHARLIE-SEVEN." Alvarez's response was breathless but audible, his voice slightly distorted by interference. "We're approximately five miles east of Balete Pass, over."

I repeated the coordinates, testing the static, then waiting anxiously for a response. As I surveyed my surroundings, I took note of the blistering sun beating down on me, creating a stifling heat from every direction, searing my skin, and sending sweat pouring down my face and back. I had to wonder where all this moisture was coming from, for by now, I was beginning to feel dehydrated too, the last thing anyone needed under these circumstances. I had to keep a rein on it; the mission and all the men needed me to stay sharp.

As fast as I drank from my water, the more the sun seemed to beat down and the more I sweated the precious resource back out. It was as if nature itself was conspiring against us. Finally, Alvarez's voice came through, slightly clearer this time.

"Copy that, Commander. Can you repeat your coordinates, over?" I pressed, trying to focus my mind and ignore such oppressive conditions. The radio fizzed and popped, making it difficult to hear yet again. "Say your location again, over."

Chewing on my lower lip, I waited as the static slowed significantly, anticipation mounting in my gut. The outside world fell away for a fleeting moment, everything surrounding me fading until the intermittent bursts of Alvarez's voice seemed to absorb me. Suddenly, his voice spoke, cutting through the tension, returning me to reality.

"Okay, men! Listen up," I shouted. "Tomorrow is it. The good news is that we are not alone in the fight. The bad news is that we just don't know what lies ahead."

I paused, looking around at each man's tired face; perhaps I had not used the best words to close my sentence, delivering uncertainty and doubt and undoing the positivity of my earlier statements. My words were falling short, and now, my men were counting on me to speak from the heart again; it was what kept them buoyed. "However, we do know we've made it this far. Together. Each of us has overcome some form of fear. And when we encounter yet more of it, we shall overcome it again."

The men started to respond to my words by standing taller and getting closer.

"We fight together, and we overcome our fears together. We will win tomorrow if we do these things. I promise you this." There was steel in my gaze, and they sensed it, replying silently with their own conviction in like manner.

Though I did not look for this as a way of confirming they understood, all the men nodded resolutely as we used the remainder of the night to prepare for tomorrow's fight.

Late in the evening, I sat down with Corporal Chen; he let out a sigh of relief and began talking about how we were just one fight away from returning home. "Tomorrow's the big day, sir. Balete Pass is it. After that, we'll go home and see our families, our loved ones. I can't wait to hold my girl. I'm not wasting any time before I start a family. And I'm also going to eat everything in the cupboards."

I smiled and laughed, watching his optimism and eagerness to marry and have kids. "You do that, Chen. I'm sure she'll say yes, and you'll have a great time."

Chen leaned forward; his eyes bright with excitement. "I hope so, sir. It's been hard being away from her. What about you, sir? Are you ready to take a leap of faith?"

I let out a small chuckle, then turned to him. "Indeed, I am! I'm going to marry that girl."

Chen grinned ear to ear. "Sounds amazing, sir. I can't wait to do the same. Maybe we'll even bump into each other at home and drink together."

I grinned back, hoping that we could indeed have that drink. "That sounds like a great idea, Chen. One more fight, and then we're off back home to our loved ones."

Chen nodded, his smile fading just a little. "Sir. We've got this. We'll make it through and be home before we know it."

I couldn't shake off my unease but tried to push it aside. After all, Chen was right.

We had one more fight. That was all.

Balete Pass

As we approached Balete Pass, the atmosphere in the platoon grew tense, the anxiety etched on my men's faces as we approached the heavily fortified enemy position. My heart hammered as we continued along the winding mountain path.

The terrain around Balete Pass was rugged and treacherous, characterized by steep mountain slopes and dense vegetation making it difficult to navigate. The Pass itself was a narrow corridor with sheer cliffs on either side, making it a perfect location for an ambush. We had to be cautious and keep our wits about us to make it through.

The radio continued chattering, bringing welcome communications from our allies to the east as we reached our position. Corporal Chen stood beside me with his binoculars fixed on the enemy location, reporting the key objectives we needed to overcome. "The enemy is heavily fortified on the east side of the Pass, sir," he said. "They have machine gun emplacements and snipers in position. We'll need to neutralize them before we can advance."

I nodded grimly, knowing it would be a tough fight. I spoke into my radio. "This is Lieutenant Grey. We have arrived at our position. We are assessing the enemy's position and preparing for our assault." We continued to exchange all essential information with them, and I could only imagine how they must have been feeling at this moment.

I gathered my men around me to keep my frustration at bay. We needed to devise a plan to counter the heavy machine guns and snipers lying in wait ahead. As I stood there, looking into the faces of each of my soldiers, their expectations were resting heavily upon me.

"Any ideas, men?" I asked, scanning their faces for any hints of inspiration.

Most looked at me blankly, but Corporal Chen said, "Sir, we could try flanking them from the mountain's east side. The terrain is rocky and would allow us to cover."

This was likely the most effective plan, but one that would also put my men in great danger. I hesitated for a moment, thinking of the risks involved.

"Chen, you think we can pull that off without losing a lot of men?" I asked him.

He looked me straight in the eye. "It's a calculated risk, but if we can take out the machine guns and snipers, we can break through their defenses and move forward."

I stared at him for a long while, pondering the options. There wasn't going to be a perfect answer to this problem, and whatever decision I made could bring devastating consequences.

Finally, I made the tough call.

"All right, everyone, listen up. Corporal Chen's plan is our best chance at success. It's risky, but we must take it to break through their defenses and make it out alive."

There were some nods of agreement, but I could equally see the concern on my men's faces. I gave them one last look before an idea struck me. We could leverage our Filipino allies who had already been reporting back to us with helpful intelligence. They could focus their attack on the enemy's position from the west while we sneaked through undetected from the southeast. This would give us the element of surprise, significantly reducing the risk of losing men.

I turned to Corporal Chen and said, "Get in touch with our Filipino allies and coordinate a joint attack from both sides. It'll distract us, allowing us to all collectively move in closer and catch them unawares."

Chen nodded, smiling. "Look at you, Lieutenant," he enthused.

I nodded back, and we quickly contacted our allies and hammered out the plan's details. It wasn't a perfect solution, but it was the best chance we had of minimizing the risk to our platoon.

Standing before my men, the adrenaline was gathering, coursing through my veins. The air was tense as my men geared up, preparing for battle. I looked across the sea of faces, each filled with resolve. These were some of the bravest and most skilled soldiers I had ever worked with.

"All right, gentlemen, listen up!" I shouted, getting their attention. "We're going into battle, and we're going to have to give it our all if we want to come out on top. Are you with me?"

A chorus of affirmative responses echoed back, each stronger than the last. We were in good hands. We quickly suited up, each pulling on flak jackets and helmets, ensuring our guns were loaded and ready to go. I could see the dogged pursuit of everything we stood for written on my men's expressions as they made their final preparations.

"Remember, our first objective is to remove their machine guns and snipers. Once we've done that, we can secure the area. It will be tough, but we can do this."

As we moved into position, my heart set off pounding loudly. We had been planning this attack for weeks, but now that we were here on the front lines of the battle of Balete Pass, the reality of it all was sinking in. The sound of gunfire resounded in the distance as our Filipino allies and our platoon began firing upon the Japanese location, causing chaos and confusion amongst the enemy. For a moment, I halted my advance, scanning the rugged terrain ahead, the memory of Lillian's sweet laughter echoing in my mind. I could feel my letter to her under my front chest plate. Only one final obstacle now stood between Lillian and me, the battle that I and my men had to fight and conquer if we my girl and I were ever to reunite.

"All right, men, let's move!" I shouted, signaling to advance.

We moved quickly through the rugged terrain, taking cover wherever we could to avoid the sniper fire raining down upon us.

We were almost near the enemy camp when the distinctive sound of an alarm started going off. The Japanese were alerted to our presence, and before we knew it, we found ourselves pinned down by a wall of gunfire from their machine gun emplacements.

"Take cover!" I shouted as we scrambled to find shelter behind the nearest rocks and trees. We returned fire as best we could, but it was difficult to determine the enemy's position through the dense fog of war.

There was a pronounced fear in some of my men's eyes, and I needed to take charge if we were to get out of this with our lives. I quickly assessed the situation, studying the terrain and our options carefully.

"All right, listen up! We're going to have to flank them from the east. Chen and Rodriguez, you two will take point. We'll provide covering fire from here," I said, pointing to a nearby boulder that would serve as a good vantage point.

Chen and Rodriguez quickly nodded, grabbing their weapons and moving to the side.

As they did so, we began covering fire, trying to keep the Japanese pinned down and distracted. For a few moments, it seemed we might make it through unscathed.

But our luck didn't hold out for long. Suddenly, all hell broke loose. The Japanese had spotted our flanking maneuver, firing upon us with renewed vigor.

Screams and shouts came as my men were hit one after the other. I gritted my teeth, determined to stay focused, to find a way through. "We have to keep pushing forward! Don't stop until we've taken out those machine guns!"

We pressed on, firing as best we could, but it seemed as though we were making no progress, as if trapped in a nightmare, unable to find a way out.

But just when things seemed darkest, a loud boom resonated from the machine gun and sniper tower. Our Filipino allies had managed to lob a grenade, stunning the Japanese.

"All right, men, this is our chance! Let's move together!" I shouted, signaling for my troops to push forward.

With renewed vigor, we began advancing once again, this time with the Filipinos by our side. In this way, we were able to gain the upper hand, charging forward, firing on the enemy with everything we had, determined to take down those machine guns no matter what.

As we got closer, my heart raced. We were almost there. Just a little closer, and we'd be in striking range.

"Go, go, go!" I shouted as we made one final, desperate push for victory.

And then, it happened.

As I watched in horror, the rocket launcher hit too close to Corporal Chen and several other men. The explosion was deafening, the shockwave slamming into my body, sending me flying backward. I scrambled, searching for any signs of life.

Calling frantically for a medic, my voice strained with emotion as I tried to keep my composure. But it was not easy, my mind willfully reverting to the plans that Chen had only shared with me earlier. His girlfriend, the love of his life, was awaiting him back home. And now, he may never get to see her again. And she would never see him and would have to piece back together the innumerable fragments of her now shattered life.

"Medic! I need a medic over there!" I yelled into my radio, my spirits sinking with each passing second as I waited for a response.

The thick smoke and dust only allowed the sight of vague shapes moving around Corporal Chen. We had to eliminate the threats closing in on them before we could assess the condition of our fallen comrade, so we fought to secure the perimeter, holding off the advancing enemy.

"Lieutenant! We need your help over here!" one of my men shouted, jolting me out of my reverie. I ran toward the sound of the voice, weapon ready. As I rounded the corner of a nearby building, four of my soldiers were engaged in a fierce battle with the enemy. They were outnumbered, the stress showing on their faces.

"We're holding them off, sir!" one shouted as they caught sight of me. "But we could use some reinforcements."

I sprang into action with a nod, taking out two enemy soldiers with expert precision. I was a skilled fighter, but memories of Chen and his plans clouded my mind, making focus difficult.

The fighting continued, the platoon and I holding off wave after wave of enemy attacks. But no matter how hard I tried, I couldn't shake the feeling that we were in trouble, that Chen was too.

At last, the fighting began to subside, and my men had managed to secure the perimeter again. They were battered and bruised, but they'd done what they had set out to do.

"Private Richardson, I need a status report on Corporal Chen," I said, my voice hoarse with emotion as I braced myself for the worst. Several minutes passed as several of my men tended to where Chen and the others were while we provided cover.

Richardson looked at me intently, his demeanor softening into a smile. "He's alive, sir," he said, his voice filled with relief. "But it looks like he has shell shock symptoms."

Unfortunately, I was all too familiar with shell shock. From my experience, most men had been knocked out or passed out from some form of explosion or a good ole-fashioned punch to the face; it was just a temporary thing but was something to monitor to ensure the man was all right and regained consciousness. I breathed a deep sigh of relief, a weight lifting off my shoulders. Chen was alive and was going to pull through. I couldn't help but smile at the thought of him making it back to his girlfriend, finally able to propose and start their life together.

And of course, in my mind, I mentally undid the appalling scene I had imagined earlier, the one in which she received the tragic news of his passing. Now, life was bright again, and I turned to my men and gave them a thumbs-up, and they let out a resounding cheer. It had been a tough battle, but we had come out on top just as I had promised them. And now, with Chen alive and on his way to recovery, it seemed nothing could stop us.

"Okay, men, let's regroup over there!" I shouted as I pointed at the first building of about a mile-long narrow road full of similar premises.

After several minutes, all of the men were near me. I looked at Chen, offering, "You've seen better days, but I'm glad to see you still upright."

He responded with his inimitable sense of humor, "Can't die before my honeymoon, Lieutenant." We all laughed at that.

The sun was beginning to dip toward the mountains as we regained our bearings, the massive packs on my soldiers' backs causing them to shuffle their feet. We fought for several hours, but the adrenaline coursing through our veins kept us going. Finally, after intense fighting, we secured the entrance to the pass, our top priority.

The strategic importance of this gateway could not be overstated, both the American and Japanese forces obviously well aware of this fact. I had to remain focused on this immediate objective and the larger picture, knowing our decisions could affect the entire campaign.

The sun was almost beneath the mountain range as my men split into small teams and began to fan out, meticulously and methodically pressing forward. Our training had been grueling, but it paid off as their battlefield tactics were finely honed, ensuring maximum safety and effectiveness.

We kept a steady stream of radio chatter with our Filipino allies, coordinating our movements and ensuring we were all on the same page. We reviewed our code words and signals to secure communication and prevent Japanese spies from intercepting our messages. The radio crackled into life more and more with ever-increasing activity as we reported on our progress, updating our allies on our movements and any new developments in the battle.

Our move was met with pockets of resistance, and we needed to use grenades and small arms fire to neutralize the enemy before pressing on. We pushed deeper into the narrow pass, engaging in difficult close quarters and exerting ourselves in a way we had not yet done in the campaign. Progress was slow, but we could not relent.

As hours dragged on, the radio traffic became even more frantic, our Filipino allies urging us to move more quickly, fearing the Japanese would regroup and mount a deadly counterattack. Despite our exhaustion and dwindling supplies, we did so, pushing to our limits, knowing full well that this mission was vital to our overall success.

After several days, we had achieved what had seemed nearly impossible, the narrow pass filling with the cheers of the Filipino soldiers as they reclaimed their land from Japanese forces. The scene was captivating, and we were all charged with emotion as we embraced each other.

Suddenly, my radio crackled to life. "CHARLIE-SEVEN, this is VICTOR. Do you copy?"

I replied crisply, "This is CHARLIE-SEVEN, loud and clear, VICTOR."

VICTOR informed me that two thousand allied soldiers would be coming through Balete Pass in the next days, our task being to ensure their safe passage. I acknowledged the message and turned to my men, informing them of our new task.

***

As we established a strong perimeter, the radio traffic continued over the coming days. Distant chatter sounded from the troops ahead of us, reporting their successes and concerns. "This is Tango Two; we have neutralized the enemy at grid reference 467169 and are moving forward."

The room fell silent as the radio crackled once more, and I brought it closer to my ear, straining to hear the message through the static. A commanding voice spoke. "You and your team are dismissed and called to return home." I could barely believe what I'd just heard.

After placing the radio down, I looked around the room, my gaze locking onto Corporal Chen, my trusted companion throughout this mission.

"I have some news," I announced, my voice loaded with both excitement and disbelief. "Our orders just arrived, and we're heading back home, Chen."

Chen tilted his head in disbelief, a glimmer of hope in his eyes.

"We're going home? Just like that?" he asked, as if waiting for someone to tell him it was a dream.

With an undeniable sense of pride, I allowed a broad smile to spread across my face as I acknowledged his words. "Absolutely. You've earned every bit of it, and so have I," I responded, a swell of accomplishment coursing through me like a surge of energy.

Stepping out of the building, I turned to Chen, a conspiratorial glint in my eyes. Leaning slightly, I lowered my voice to a whisper. "Oh, and speaking of promotions, don't think I forgot about you. Congratulations."

Chen's eyes widened in pleasant shock, a mix of surprise and excitement washing over his features. In an instant, he snapped to attention, offering a crisp and precise salute. Then, with a chuckle, he added, "Well, that's good news. I was starting to think I'd have to sell my soul to pay for that engagement ring!" Our shared laughter echoed in testament to the camaraderie that had grown between us during all our shared experiences.

The passing weeks and months brought about a continuation of challenges and triumphs, the bond between Chen and me deepening with each shared obstacle we overcame. We celebrated victories together, supported each other through setbacks, and found solace in each other's presence during moments of quiet reflection.

Our interactions weren't confined to the battlefield alone, however. We also explored the local surroundings, shared stories of our lives back home, and even managed to engage in a few friendly competitions, adding an element of friendly rivalry to our partnership.

As time went on, the remaining two months felt like a blur, a whirlwind of shared laughter, late-night conversations, and mutual encouragement. Our newfound friendship grew stronger, our understanding of each other deepening beyond the confines of duty.

Through it all, Chen's impending departure hung in the back of our minds, an inevitable reality that we did our best to ignore. When the day for him to leave finally arrived, there was an undeniable sense of bittersweetness. As we stood there, preparing to bid each other farewell, all the tension of our impending separation was palpable. Our embrace was tighter than ever now, reflecting the depth of our connection.

"Stay safe, Chen," I murmured, my voice a mixture of reassurance and a tinge of sadness. "And don't forget to keep me updated on everything, especially the big moment," I added with a playful grin, referring to the proposal he had planned. "Send me an invitation to the wedding, won't you?"

Chen returned the hug with equal warmth, a nostalgic glint in his eyes as he nodded enthusiastically. "I promise, I'll make sure to give you all the details," he responded, his voice delivering a heartfelt sincerity.

As we finally pulled away from each other, I couldn't help but feel a swell of emotion. The two months we had spent together had more than solidified our bond, turning us from fellow soldiers into true friends. Despite the physical distance that would soon separate us, the memories we had created would remain a cherished part of both our lives.

The memories of those intense months still lingered, a testament to the strength of the connections forged in the crucible of conflict. In a world in which time had surged forward, the camaraderie between Chen and me remained a constant, a beacon of friendship that had withstood the test of time.

Several hours later I stood outside an old, white-washed farmhouse, holding firmly onto a letter. Beads of sweat trickled down my back, racing to the ground as I lifted my hat and combed my hand through my hair. As I stepped onto the cozy and spacious wrap-around porch, my heart pounded deeper as I took one last long look at my military service dress.

Approaching the door, I took a deep breath and then knocked. After several long seconds, footsteps sounded from inside. I gripped the letter tightly.

The door opened, and I called out softly, "Lillian?"

PART THREE:

THE MUSTANG

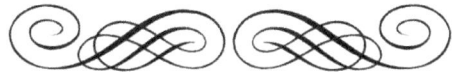

Trial by Fire

In the scorching heat of the desert, Al Udeid Air Base stood as a beacon of American airpower, bringing a new challenge for me. Stepping into the base in Qatar felt as though I had ventured into an inferno. The sun beat down with unyielding intensity, while the air was chokingly humid, the heat seeming to seep through every pore of my body. A shimmering haze hung over the horizon, blurring the boundaries between the golden desert and its azure sky.

As I walked through the outer corridors, my mind began wandering to all that lay ahead. After all, I was embarking on a new chapter of my military career, the promotion a remarkable achievement considering how far I had come, from first enlisting as one of few female airmen to now becoming a flight commander. It was only natural to feel anxious, but I drew in a deep breath, summoning my will to tackle the challenges of this new role with unwavering resolve.

With a sense of relief, I stepped into my office, grateful for its cool blast of air-conditioning that enveloped my tired body. A sigh escaped my lips as I settled into the chair behind the desk, positioned at the center of the room.

I couldn't help but admire the professional yet austere atmosphere. The wooden plaques, stacks of files, and the standard military computer had all been carefully placed on the desk, contributing to the purposeful ambiance of this space. The walls were adorned with large maps showcasing different strategic points, each one meticulously highlighted and marked.

It was evident that this office held an essential role in some complex operations. My eyes wandered over the maps, the sight unleashing both excitement and responsibility; I had big shoes to fill, especially considering the previous occupant's outstanding work.

As I began to sort through the files on the desk, my initial enthusiasm waned. There were no turnover documents to be found, and the absence of notes explaining the files or the markings on the maps was puzzling. *I'll check out the tall drawer cabinet beside the desk,* I said to myself, hoping to find some hidden cache of information. But, to my dismay, the drawers contained only general office supplies—pens, staples, and a hole punch—and not a single turnover document.

Frustration was mounting by the second.

I continued to search through the files on the desk, hoping that maybe I had overlooked something. But the situation remained the same—no context, no guidance. It seemed as if the responsibility of understanding the intricacies of this office fell entirely upon my shoulders.

Though the situation was less than ideal, it also presented an opportunity for me to test my skills and capability. Driven by determination, I took the challenge and scavenged the computer that soon proved to be a treasure trove of information, containing numerous email exchanges and crucial documents. With each piece I analyzed, I began gaining footing amidst the mess.

To bring some semblance of order to the confusion, I turned my attention back to the tall drawer cabinet. There, I unearthed a stack of sticky notes and a pen to aid in my task of making sense of the maps. Starting with the base's layout, I carefully studied the aerial view, gradually working my way through the other maps which were more intricate and technical in nature. It was a laborious process in which perhaps not everything became crystal clear, but I at least managed to piece together enough to glean from the snippets some level of understanding.

Continuing my exploration of the office, my eyes were drawn to a massive whiteboard placed right behind my desk. It stood tall on a mobile stand with wheels. Inspiration struck and I decided to use it to create a list of tasks, the perfect way to organize my thoughts and prioritize my actions big and bold. I couldn't claim to have overlooked my list if I wrote it for all to see.

But before I could start writing things down, a voice interrupted.

Turning around, I found John Garcia, an experienced and reliable flight chief, standing by the door. Before my arrival at Al Udeid, I had made sure to take the initiative and reach out to him. With his impressive eighteen years of experience as a master sergeant, it was plainly crucial to have a seasoned senior NCO by my side in this unfamiliar territory.

John Garcia's reputation preceded him, and I was eager to work with someone so reputedly sharp, experienced, and wholly dedicated to his work.

His black hair, neatly combed back, added an air of sophistication to his appearance, contrasting the haphazard appearance of many aspects of our new environment. His composed demeanor acted as a calming balm, soothing the nerves that had been on edge since stepping foot in this unfamiliar place. Despite not being physically imposing, an undeniable aura of strength and wisdom surrounded him, putting me instantly at ease.

"Just came to check in," he said softly, his eyes wandering across the room, taking in the sight of the newly claimed office. "How are you holding up?" Genuine concern was evident in his tone.

"The heat's unbearable, but I'll manage," I replied swiftly, gently placing the marker back down onto the desk. "I suppose air conditioning throughout is too much to ask for."

He chuckled. "The heat can be brutal at times. It takes some getting used to."

"Hmm, I certainly agree with you there," I said, glancing out the window at the scorching landscape beyond the cool walls of my office. "But I must admit, I don't envy the airmen working outside in this."

John's expression turned somber, a tinge of woe perhaps.

"Speaking of our airmen, we have a problem," he uttered.

My heart sank, bracing myself for some unsettling news. "Why? What's going on?"

"Two of our airmen in Iraq have been wounded in an attack," he informed, his voice laden with concern.

"What happened?" I asked, trying to comprehend the severity of the situation.

John let out a sigh. "Airmen Lee and Foster were at the smoke pit when a mortar hit nearby. The situation is being closely monitored."

My stomach twisted with worry. "Are they okay?"

"We're still awaiting news from the medical team on the ground," John replied. "I'll continue to pass updates as I receive them."

"Thank you, John," I managed to say, doing my best to steady my voice in the face of such deeply troubling news.

His eyes full of worry, he swept from the room after nodding understandingly, leaving me to pace the office, my mind racing with thoughts and plans.

"Looks like I'll be meeting the commander earlier than expected," I whispered to myself, inadvertently taking upon myself so much more than I knew how to carry.

Due to my efforts and proactive approach with the maps, I easily navigated through the base, making my way to the squadron headquarters building. Of course, as a seasoned member of the military, I was accustomed to operating in deployed settings in which every structure had been designed to withstand harsh conditions. The headquarters building was no exception.

Solidly constructed from sand-colored bricks blending seamlessly with the desert surroundings, the building's appearance gave a sense of reassurance amidst the blistering heat. Its sturdy metal roof provided protection from the unforgiving sun, while its vast windows brought in much-needed natural light. Inside, the cool air conditioning offered a momentary respite from those relentless desert temperatures.

Upon stepping inside, I was immediately impressed by the well-maintained and organized appearance. Freshly painted walls, gleaming floors, and bright lights reflected the dedication of the maintenance team in keeping these particular premises impeccable. Despite its functional layout, the building managed to create an atmosphere of warmth and camaraderie. The open-plan office arrangement encouraged collaboration and teamwork, everywhere buzzing with activity, phones ringing, and the friendly chatter of fellow airmen.

I made my way to the front desk. Here, I was warmly greeted by a friendly airman who kindly directed me to Lieutenant Colonel Peterson's office.

Walking into the squadron commander's office was one of the most daunting tasks I had encountered since joining the Air Force. As a woman in a predominantly male-dominated field, I already carried the weight of proving myself, and now, with two wounded airmen—Airman Lee and Airman Foster—under my charge, this meeting held critical significance.

Squadron Commander Lieutenant Colonel Peterson sat at his desk, already dressed in his uniform. His presence was imposing, his broad chest and square jawline exuding strength. Despite his formidable appearance, there was a sense of calm and assurance about him that made me feel as if he was someone I could instinctively trust.

"Captain Norah Katz?" he asked, extending his hand in a gesture of greeting. "Yes, sir. It's an honor to meet you," I replied, shaking his hand respectfully. "Sir, I am here to inform you about Airmen Lee and Foster. They have been wounded in a mortar attack in Iraq. Fortunately, they are receiving local medical treatment," I explained.

The commander's eyes widened with surprise and concern, clearly affected. "I am sorry to hear that, Captain," he responded with genuine sorrow. "We'll do everything we can to support their families and ensure they receive the necessary medical care."

"Thank you, sir," I replied, appreciating his immediate concern for the welfare of our injured airmen.

"I'll inform the wing commander about this," he said before continuing, "Captain, I'm sure you're already aware, but this will be a challenging time for all of us. The injury of any of our comrades is taken very seriously."

Relieved at his support, I let out a small sigh.

"Don't worry," he added. "I'm here to support you as a new member of this team." A supportive smile graced his expression.

Greatly set at ease by his words, I nodded gratefully and decided to make my way back to my office. The news had been unsettling but knowing that the Commander had my back and that the injured airmen would be receiving all the necessary care provided some comfort amidst the uncertainty. As I walked back, I reminded myself of the importance of being a steadfast leader and providing support to my team during these challenging times.

After returning to my office and refocusing on my previous commitments, another interruption came in the form of a sudden knock on the door. I swiveled in the chair, watching as the handle slowly depressed to reveal a tall man. *No idea who this is,* I thought.

He was quite impressive, with his tall stature and hair loosely gelled back, though the sweltering heat seemed to defy any attempts at keeping it in place; I was momentarily glad not to wear makeup at work, since no doubt by now, it would also have been sliding down my cheeks.

Clad in a crisp flight suit, the man exuded sophistication and authority.

For a moment, I stood there, silently assessing the newcomer to my office before he cleared his throat and spoke. "I am so sorry to bother you, but I am in need of some assistance."

"Certainly, and you are?" I replied, more than a hint of uncertainty in my voice.

"My name's Brian Solomon," he said, extending his hand forward. "Captain Brian Solomon."

"It's a pleasure to meet you, Captain," I replied, shaking his hand. "What can I help you with?"

He sheepishly rubbed his neck and said, "Um, I can't seem to turn on my computer, and I don't know how to fix it. I heard you could help with that."

Inside my mind, I giggled.

Really? This statuesque figure, a captain, doesn't even know how to bring his computer to life?

Of course, technology was not everyone's forte, but a more than basic knowledge of IT was expected for such a role. Turning on a computer, I thought, came right at the bottom of the tasks requiring mastery or expert knowledge. But I was careful not to let my pent-up giggle emerge, for I didn't wish to embarrass someone I didn't yet know. He also looked very serious.

"Of course, lead the way," I said, happy to offer my assistance.

It was true what he'd said. Everyone claimed I had a gift for all things technological, so no doubt someone who couldn't be bothered to assist him had instinctively inserted my name into the conversation when computer issues had popped up as a barrier.

We walked to Captain Solomon's office, which was nearby but turned out to be distinctly neater than mine, adorned with small ornaments and trinkets on a clean and polished desk. Of course, it also held the usual dark hardwood photo frames with pictures of the family. As we approached the desk, he reached forward and swiveled his large monitor to face me better, wafting his hand over it with an air of slight frustration. "So, everything seems to be on and working, but the screen just isn't responding. It's just pitch black, as you can see," he explained. "Suppose I should've said it wasn't a computer issue so much as a screen one. Would this still fall into your area of expertise?"

I observed the situation for a moment, nodding to confirm I could fix it, yet still trying not to chuckle at the captain's cluelessness. My hands reached for the power button, and with a few seconds of pressing and resetting, the screen sprang to life, revealing a bright and garish wallpaper with a funny quote.

He laughed off his embarrassment, a smile crossing his face for the first time.

"Ahh, I see. So that's what it was," he proclaimed. "Now, why didn't I do that?"

"They're pretty much all the same," I said, shrugging with a smile. "All a bit temperamental. If in doubt, just turn off at the outlet, then on again, and rinse and repeat. Of course, check you have the on button pressed at the side or back of the monitor as well."

I hoped my utterance about the devices' moodiness made him feel better about his ineptitude.

"If it weren't for you, I would've been stuck here staring at the screen," he said gratefully.

"Oh, anytime. It was no trouble at all," I reassured him. "Any other tech problems, Captain?"

"No, no, thank you. I think the computer works just fine." He then surprised me with a friendly offer. "I was wondering if you would care to join me for dinner at the chow hall. Let's say it's my way of showing my appreciation."

As a newcomer to the base with limited acquaintances, this was a welcomed invitation, and I quickly nodded. "I would love to."

With a genuine smile, Captain Brian Solomon extended his hospitality.

With a return grin of my own, I had been thrilled to accept, believing this impromptu dinner would not only offer me a chance to unwind but would also present a wonderful opportunity to forge a new friendship in this challenging yet exciting environment.

After parting ways with him, I returned to my office where Master Sergeant Garcia warmly greeted me. Approaching, I couldn't help but ask anxiously, "Sergeant Garcia, any updates on Airman Lee and Airman Foster? It's hard not to worry for them."

With a reassuring smile, he responded confidently, "Yes, ma'am. Both airmen are safe and sound. The medical team is assessing them, but it seems they're doing well."

My heart leaped with joy, and I breathed a deep sigh of relief. Grateful for Master Sergeant Garcia's diligent efforts, I appreciated his dedication in keeping me informed during such critical moments. As he held his phone, offering to make a call, he said, "I have their phone numbers. Would you like to speak to them?"

I gratefully nodded, eager to hear directly from my brave airmen. "Of course. Put them on speakerphone, please," I requested, wanting them to know my gratitude for their courage.

As Airman Lee's voice came through, I sensed his surprise, perhaps mildly shocked to hear a woman's voice. However, he quickly composed himself and gave an update. "I'm doing okay, ma'am. It was scary, but we came through it."

I let out a chuckle, trying to put him at ease. "No apologies necessary, Airman Lee. I'm just glad you're both safe."

Airman Foster echoed similar sentiments, "I'm a bit shaken up but happy the alarm went off."

As they bade me farewell, I couldn't help but express my pride and joy for their bravery under duress. "I'm so proud of you both. Now, take care and focus on your recovery," I urged, wanting them to know that their well-being was my utmost priority. "Take the time you need."

Once the call ended, I turned to Master Sergeant Garcia, his swift action and quick response in my mind. "Thank you for your dedication and handling the situation promptly. We dodged a bullet there," I acknowledged, fully aware of the potential outcome's severity had he been less attentive.

As I settled back into my office chair, a profound sense of gratitude swelled my heart for the skilled and caring team surrounding me. With Master Sergeant Garcia by my side, I could navigate through any challenges that lay ahead, confident in the knowledge that our airmen were in good hands and that we would overcome whatever obstacles came our way.

I stood up, seeking solace in the mirror hanging on the wall. My reflection displayed a petite, five-foot-three woman, resembling my beloved grandmother whom I had always admired. Despite the rigidity of my hair tied in a military bun, my brunette locks reflected the same elegance she also possessed. My eyes, an intriguing shade of green with a unique hazel undertone, had been a gift from my maternal grandfather, looking much like his own.

As memories of Basic Military Training in San Antonio, Texas, flooded my mind, I couldn't help but feel unsure yet full of anticipation. My well-pressed uniform, painstakingly perfected through countless hours of effort, symbolized my commitment to this new life chapter. However, my pride in achieving that level of precision was tempered by the realization that the uniform had not been designed with women's bodies in mind. It chafed, sitting close in all the wrong places, also restricting my movement far more than I would have liked.

Oh, what I'd give for a pair of stretchy elasticated pants, I thought, snickering quietly.

Nonetheless, I found strength in the legacy of my grandmother, a woman of quiet and pensive mien whose actions spoke louder than words. Like her, I was among the first women—in fact, only the second—in my family to serve in the military, and I was aware of drawing upon her spirit to navigate the unique challenges I faced as a female airman.

Reflecting on the progress we had made since the early days of female military service, I found solace in knowing that we had come a long way. Proudly serving in this esteemed institution, I stood as a testament to the bold strides we women had made, heralding the potential for our even greater progress in the future. While the shortcomings of our scratchy and restrictive uniforms were disheartening, they were also a welcomed reminder of the work that remained to ensure gender equality and inclusivity within the military.

Yet despite the challenges, my dedication and commitment to serving my country remained in place. My value as an airman extended far beyond what uniform I wore, and I was determined to make a difference to the lives of those alongside whom I served.

Turning away from the mirror with a fond, bright smile, my thoughts drifted back to one of the most momentous occasions of my life so far, the day on which I had been officially sworn in as an airman. The memory of taking the oath of allegiance still filled me with immense pride and a sense of accomplishment. However, a hint of sadness also accompanied the recollection, knowing it was one of the last times my family had gathered together. Life had taken us all along different paths, such rare moments of togetherness now cherished deeply.

In the midst of these reflections, a renewed sense of purpose was emerging. My journey as a female airman was not just about personal achievement; it was also about breaking barriers and creating a more inclusive and diverse military for future generations. With the legacy of my grandmother and the support of those who believed in me, I was ready to face the challenges ahead with whatever it took, committing to making a difference.

Shaking off those nostalgic feelings, I refocused my mind on the present. Determined to make the most of my first day on base, I decided to dive into the tasks at hand. I started by sorting out documents and folders on the computer, organizing them with a newfound sense of purpose.

As I picked up momentum, my fingers flew across the keyboard, swiftly combing through tasks that needed my attention. The sense of accomplishment was growing with each item I could check off my list. By the end of the day, a great sense of satisfaction and pride filled me; I had managed to cover a significant amount of ground, setting a strong foundation for my work in the days to come. After this, I stood up to stretch, only to hear a knock on the door.

It opened, Captain Solomon stepping inside.

"I hope I'm not intruding," he said, watching me work.

"No, not at all. How may I help you?" I asked with a small smile.

"Well, if it's not too much to ask, I would like to ask you to walk with me to the chow hall for dinner," he replied with a chuckle. "If we don't leave soon, we will be getting leftovers." He turned his wrist, checking the time.

My head whipped toward the wall, also eyeing the large clock, aghast. Had I really been so wrapped up in work? "Oh, I didn't notice," I said, standing. "Really sorry! But I appreciate the wake-up call. And besides, it's very gentlemanly to pick up the lady for dinner."

We laughed. "It's not as if we have to travel far," he said. "Thankfully so. Anyway, you're welcome. It's the least I can do."

As we started walking toward the chow hall, the sun hung low, the base growing enveloped in long shadows. The scorching heat was still evident but was thankfully feeling somewhat less oppressive now as we strolled side by side.

Captain Brian Solomon had a knack for keeping the conversation light and engaging. "You know, they say you can cook an egg on the pavements here," he chuckled, pointing at the sunbaked ground. "I haven't tried it yet, but I've seen some folks get pretty creative with their experiments! If we've already missed dinner, perhaps we could try it. Do you have a couple of eggs on you by chance?"

I shook my head no, giggling aloud, appreciating his lightheartedness. "Well, let's add that to our to-do list, shall we? Cooking eggs in the Qatar heat," I teased playfully. "Next time you collect me from my room, I will bring eggs."

"Sounds like a plan!" he replied with a grin, his eyes twinkling with mirth. "But on a serious note, how are you settling in? I know it can be overwhelming at first, but you'll get the hang of it soon enough."

"It's definitely been like a tornado," I admitted, grateful for the chance to share my thoughts with Captain Solomon. "But having someone like you to show me the ropes has been a great help. I appreciate it. You think I'm the one who did you a favor, but you can't know how much it applies in reverse."

Captain Solomon's response was warm and reassuring. "Hey, that's what we're here for, to support each other. Besides, it's always nice to see new faces around this place. Keeps things interesting. Anyway, if it hadn't been for you, I'd still be trying to switch on my screen. Probably would have been stuck there all night."

He chuckled again.

As I nodded and laughed in agreement, we continued walking toward the hall. But just before we could step inside, Captain Solomon turned his body to face me with a playful expression. A sheepish smile adorned his face. "I don't know if it's too late to ask, but may I know your name?"

I couldn't help but chuckle at his candidness. "Oh! How remiss of me not to have told you. Of course, it's Norah, Norah Katz."

"Norah," he repeated, as if savoring the sound of my name. "It's beautiful."

His compliment caught me by surprise, a slight blush creeping onto my cheeks. "Thank you," I replied, appreciating the unexpected and genuine compliment.

Finally stepping inside the chow hall, the lively atmosphere of airmen already gathering for dinner greeted us. Captain Solomon held open the door with a gallant gesture, and we stepped inside. The clatter of trays, the hum of conversation, and the hubbub of chattering and laughter assaulted our hearing as we found a spot to sit together, over in a quieter corner.

As we settled into our seats after picking up the trays laden with our meals, Captain Solomon flashed a mischievous grin, his eyes twinkling almost as if it had triggered a memory. "You know, I once had a comrade who was notorious for eating his meal in record time. We called him 'Speedy Gonzales.' Don't know how he always managed to down his food so quickly, but he sure kept us entertained during chow time!"

I chuckled, amused by the nickname and the camaraderie it represented. "It sounds like he had a real talent for devouring meals. But I hope he didn't forget to enjoy the taste while breaking those records!"

"I doubt it," Captain Solomon laughed. "But, you know, these are the kinds of memories that stick with you, don't you think? The people you serve with become like family. We share the good times and the tough, and they're what inspire us to keep going, to push ourselves harder."

His words struck a chord, and I nodded in agreement. "Absolutely. It's incredible how the bond among military personnel can transcend the challenges we all face. We're united by our love and respect for the brave, the resilience and strength they exhibit every day."

Captain Solomon's eyes lit up, reflecting his passion for the military and the people who served in it. "You've got it! That's exactly why I joined, to become a part of something greater, to serve alongside others sharing the same values and sense of duty."

Religion and faith were topics that came up naturally in our conversation. Captain Solomon also mentioned that he was a proud Christian, and I shared that I, too, held my faith close to my heart. We talked about how our beliefs provided us with the necessary strength and guidance in both our personal and professional lives, and I found it comforting to find a shared spiritual connection, a common thread drawing us even closer together.

As the evening sun painted the cloudless sky with hues of orange and pink, we wrapped up our mealtime and started walking back to our respective offices. The bond between us had deepened, strengthened by shared experiences and common values.

"I'm so glad we had this chance to connect," Captain Solomon said warmly. "It's not every day you find someone with whom you can share such meaningful conversations."

"I feel the same way," I replied, touched by his sincerity. "It's a privilege to have you as a friend and fellow airman."

With a shared sense of optimism for the days to come, we parted ways, each of us carrying a newfound excitement for the challenges and adventures that lay ahead.

With a friend like Captain Solomon by my side, my military journey would be enriched and filled with meaningful connections, all in service to something greater than themselves, no matter the heat of the fire in which I found myself.

An Unseen Burden

A few mornings later, I awoke to be momentarily taken aback by unfamiliar surroundings.

The tent in which I found myself bore a resemblance to the one I had grown accustomed to, only with a few subtle upgrades.

Perhaps this added comfort was an expected perk accompanying my promotion.

My body had grown accustomed to the brisk routine of waking during ungodly early hours of the morning, a practice ingrained in me, even in these new surroundings. So, it felt just right to be taking a nice casual stroll on my way to the office.

As the sun lingered just below the horizon, the sky was transforming into a mesmerizing canvas, blending the remnants of night with the emerging strokes of a golden dawn. A refreshing breeze was dancing over the surroundings, sending a few dried-up leaves skittering along parched earth, the slight wind a more-than-pleasant contrast to the sweltering afternoon that lay ahead.

Upon returning to my office, a surge of purpose was propelling me toward the whiteboard once again. This time, however, I was determined to draft a comprehensive list of priorities. The previous day had proven somewhat productive, yet the scope of my responsibilities as a flight commander remained considerable, and the luxury of failure was one I couldn't afford. However, although resolute in my pursual of greatness, it was exactly those ambitions and expectations that repeatedly held me back from excelling, something I found infuriating.

The fear of failure and shame brought about unsettling feelings of anxiety that would sometimes consume me. I had to get a grip on these if I were ever to make the kind of progress I was looking for, yet time and again, my nerves would fail me under pressure.

My existence as an airman, firmly entrenched in the folds of the military, bound me to never showcase my weakness, something especially important as a female. The last thing any woman airman would wish for was to be labeled weak or moody, so any display of such fragility was not only undesirable but also shameful, to be swiftly met with unease and retribution. Against all my better judgment, there were so many times in which I would wonder, *how would a male airman approach this problem?* But how could I possibly know? Besides, we were all individuals, no two airmen seeing an issue exactly the same way. Gender didn't come into it.

Thus, this battle of my wits was one I had to fight and conquer alone; no one could really help me in the struggle against my own self-doubts and recriminations.

I shook my head, attempting to dispel all these negative and pervasive thoughts from piling up inside of me. Just then, a knock on the door interrupted, followed by the entrance of Master Sergeant Garcia.

"Hey, settling into the place?" he inquired, a smile gracing his lips.

"I suppose," I responded, briefly acknowledging him before redirecting my focus back to the task at hand, organizing my duties on the board. I felt my brow furrow as if by its own will, but I really did want a good, clear shot at sorting everything once and for all. "Is there something you need to discuss?" I asked, aware it sounded a little terse. "I'm a bit tied up as you can see."

Garcia shook his head, his expression earnest. "Nothing of that sort really, so don't mind me. I'm just curious—what's on your agenda?"

"Attempting to devise a plan for tackling my responsibilities. Plus, I still need to formally meet some team members and section chiefs, establish connections," I explained, my thoughts partially consumed by the task of translating my intentions onto the whiteboard. I never had been skilled at writing on such a surface, feeling somewhat self-conscious whenever I had to present written points before a group. The presentation part was fine, but my writing just refused to comply on the large format. Trying to plan out my work tasks in this way served the dual purpose of trying to perfect my writing on this awkward surface.

I rubbed out some of what I had drafted, intent on redoing that segment.

Before the marker even touched the whiteboard, however, Garcia interjected once again. "Well, there's no time like the present. Strategies can wait. Your board will still be here later."

"Oh, but I really should—"

John interjected again. "Believe me, after this initial phase, you'll have ample time to work on your strategies. Presently, there are no pressing cases or missions. This is your prime opportunity to introduce yourself to everyone. Come, I'll aid you."

With John's persuasion, I found myself being drawn out of my office, compelled to interact with various individuals within teams and across the base. Our initial plan had been to head to the main lobby until we stumbled upon Sergeant Sands, the Server Section Chief, while traversing the base camp. Contrary to my expectations, Sergeant Sands did not fit the stereotypical mold I had in mind for someone of his background.

I should have known far better than to succumb to the cliché of expecting all military personnel to appear rugged and battle-hardened. To put it simply, he looked like Santa Claus, short and squat in stature, pleasantly plump, and sporting a perpetually jolly expression with kind eyes that crinkled. Well, let's say he was Santa minus the white hair and long scraggly beard. And as far as I could observe, he had not come bearing gifts.

His demeanor matched his appearance, exuding a cheerful and delightful disposition.

Despite our all-too-brief interaction, it was evident that he was a conversationalist whose phraseology and delivery accurately mirrored his jolly, reddened visage. During our exchange, I discovered he was enroute to supervise the delivery of security patches to our classified systems, protocols to prevent users from corrupting anything or allowing in malware.

Our brief conversation turned out to be a genuine pleasure, revealing more of his amiable nature and fostering a sense of camaraderie. As our paths diverged, he even extended a warm invitation to a cup of coffee. Politely declining the offer, I excused myself, and he graciously understood.

Getting back on track, we ended up at the main lobby where we engaged in a brief exchange of words with a friendly airman, the same one who had helped me on my first day on base. I came to learn his name was Samuel Boyd, although he adamantly preferred the more casual moniker "Sam." Typically stationed behind the front desk, he tirelessly assisted everyone in navigating the base's many intricacies. He was very young and full of vigor, and I found it refreshing seeing such driving ambition in a young fellow.

With Sam's guidance, we embarked on the next leg of our journey, ultimately reaching the IT help desk where we met Technical Sergeant Cothran. After exchanging necessary pleasantries, our conversation was to be short, given his apparent immersion in an ocean of files and an incessantly ringing, annoying telephone.

As I strolled away from the lobby, my gaze happened upon Captain Solomon, or rather *Brian.* This was the name I was aware he preferred in our informal moments, a preference that had grown out of our frequent dinner rendezvous by now. Notably, this casual familiarity was something I relished, finding comfort in our shared meals and engaging conversations. Despite our paths intersecting right now, however, our eyes didn't meet, and I silently observed his entrance into the bustling lobby. A strong urge was welling within me though, tempting me to call out a friendly greeting or even approach him. Yet a sense of duty and responsibility prevailed, grounding me in the reality of my obligations.

Accompanied by Sergeant Garcia, therefore, I continued my stride, eventually arriving at the office of Staff Sergeant James, a man entrusted with overseeing the Network Section. As I entered, I noted an ongoing discussion between Staff Sergeants James and Chacon, Chief of the Radio Section. Their conversation centered on enhancing the infrastructure, with a focus on installing a new mass notification system.

During their conversation, Staff Sergeants James and Chacon were taking turns introducing one another, an interaction that caught my attention and delighted me. Their shared connection was evident and uplifting, likely fostered by their collaboration amidst the challenges faced by both of their equally understaffed work centers.

Staff Sergeant James acknowledged Chacon's expertise in radio operations, recognizing his role as a dependable source of communication support. This highlighted their collaboration in a professional context in which Chacon's skills directly addressed the communication hurdles both men were daily encountering.

Staff Sergeant Chacon reciprocated by acknowledging Staff Sergeant James' own strengths and accomplishments, again most pleasing to hear and witness. Their mutual regard appeared to be grounded in a deep respect for each other's competencies, something which could serve as a valuable asset when navigating complex decisions in the future.

As we made our way back to my office, a thought escaped my lips. "This turned out to be a wonderful idea."

John glanced my way, curiosity glinting in his gaze. "What idea?"

"Stepping out of the confines of my office and connecting with the people I'll be collaborating with," I explained. "There's an indescribable sense of contentment in being here. The competencies and skills everyone shows are reassuring. It's hard to fathom a day that won't unfold seamlessly with all these talented people aboard."

Gazing back at the individuals I'd had the privilege to meet, each distinct and resolute in their purpose, I couldn't help but marvel. Together, they resembled a harmonious ensemble, a united force working in tandem. I reiterated my gratitude, turning to John with a sincere smile. "Thank you, John. This truly was brilliant advice. I think I'll feel a lot more confident around the place now you've shown me who's who."

A momentary smile appeared on John's lips, his reply tender. "Always a pleasure." With that, his hand rested lightly on the back of my shoulder as he ushered me back through a doorway toward my own office. "See," he said on our return. "Didn't I tell you that whiteboard wasn't going anywhere? There she stands, still awaiting your attention."

"And what makes you think it's a *she?*" I quipped, picking him up on his wording.

I laughed heartily. It was true, however, that getting out had done me a considerable service. To think that I could have spent that time alone in my room and missed out on the opportunity to which John had just treated me. Truly, a sense of gratitude was burning in me; I felt a far greater sense of belonging now I could put names to faces and tasks.

The day unexpectedly seemed to draw to a close ahead of schedule, an uncommon occurrence that left me with a peculiar sense of achievement. Strangely, a fair share of credit belonged to Sergeant Garcia for orchestrating this newfound ease.

As I reflected back on the day, my thoughts drifted back to the moment of crossing paths with Captain Solomon. Contemplating our brief encounter, I wondered whether I should have mustered a gesture, even just a friendly wave.

It felt cold having just passed by one another without saying anything at all, yet the thought of doing something seemed foolish, given the circumstances. We had been strolling in opposite directions, and he hadn't even met my gaze. I could only have resorted to walking up to him and tapping his shoulder, if not calling out his name to get his attention. Regrettably, both actions appeared less than appropriate, potentially disrupting his professional stride. After all, he was engrossed in his own professional undertakings, just as I had been absorbed in mine. Interfering with his journey would have been unjust to us both.

Later in the day, however, a message arrived from him, regretfully informing me that he would not be able to accompany me to dinner tonight. A pang of disappointment cleaved through my senses, yet I understood the duty staking a priority claim on his time. The rapid cadence of our lives, dictated by demanding obligations, had cast a shadow over our usual dinner rendezvous. Now, it appeared that he too had become ensnared in the relentless grip of duty.

In our conversations, he would often weave jests to dissolve awkwardness or tension, even playfully threatening to break his computer if it meant he could come see me. While his humorous intentions warmed my heart, they also left behind a bittersweet residue, a persistent yearning for a connection not fully realized, at least not yet. Nevertheless, it was useless to hope, our paths seeming confined to separate corners within the base.

An intangible yearning lingered nevertheless, a hollowness borne of his absence, or perhaps a deeper ache stirring beneath the surface of my newfound comfort.

Within the day's wake lingered a shadow of disquiet, a spectral whisper skating through the air like an ominous harbinger. Rumors, like phantoms, coiled around us, their tendrils hinting at something dangerous, something foreboding. The very mention of the words sent an involuntary shiver down my spine, an unspoken premonition nestling itself deep within my thoughts.

The whispers were like ethereal ghosts, murmuring caution, casting veiled allusions to the possibility of retreat, even evacuation. Those terms oppressed me, stirring much malaise. In the delicate dance of this war, the tapestry of political alliances stood poised on a precipice, fragile threads that could fray and splinter under so many pivotal decisions.

As an airman, duty beckoned me to heed any command coming my way. Yet my resolve did little to quell the rising tide of anxious uncertainty. If the world around us were to tremor and crumble, if the carefully woven fabric of our reality were to unravel, there would still be the need to know, to understand it all. I couldn't remain in the dark, not when the stakes were this high.

As night descended, I sought refuge in sleep, yet my mind remained a battlefield of entangled possibilities and uncharted choices. The darkness seemed to magnify the burden of my limited knowledge, a constant reminder of the gaps in my comprehension. The realization that my control over the situation was limited only intensified the immense burden of apprehension.

My duty would be to comply with what I was given and to make it work, my commitment extending beyond my own survival, encompassing the collective well-being of my team. This, I knew, was a responsibility I would bear, come what may.

The tranquil routine of the base began like any other morning.

As the sun rose, a sense of normalcy prevailed.

Airmen in a steady stream, all clad in PT gear, made their way to the gym for their morning workout, others gathering in the bustling mess hall for breakfast.

Amidst the clatter of trays and friendly banter, a hushed anticipation was cloaking everything. The usual hum of conversations seemed muted, as if an unspoken premonition lingered on everyone's mind. As the airmen exchanged greetings and hellos, a solemn undertone hinted.

Yes, there was something amiss.

In an unexpected turn, the tranquil ambiance of the breakfast hall was abruptly shattered as silence fell. The muted hum of conversation faded abruptly into the background, replaced by the crackling resonance of a familiar voice. Through the screens mounted on the walls, a middle-aged male news anchor's solemn expression came into view, the gravitas of his words instantly capturing the attention of every individual present.

"Ladies and gentlemen," the anchor's voice proclaimed in somber cadence. "We interrupt your regular programming for an urgent update. This is CNN with breaking news. The United States has declared a non-combatant evacuation from Afghanistan."

The words emitted a shockwave, then sent it spreading through the mess hall. The few conversations that had been remaining now dwindled to a stunned silence as the announcement sank in. Murmurs of disbelief flitted through the crowd like ripples on a pond disturbed by a sudden stone's throw.

Nearby, however, a group of confident and ebullient airmen seated at a corner table engaged in fervent discussion, their voices rising slightly above the now subdued hum, opinions clashing like opposing forces on a battleground of ideas. "I can't believe they're actually pulling out," one young airman said, his tone a mix of frustration and incredulity.

His companion, more senior, shook his head. "Yeah, it's a tough call. But it's not just about us, is it? There are so many factors at play. You have to realize that."

As the debate of the two continued, other nearby airmen turned their heads, curious glances exchanged as they caught snippets of the talk. The unfolding events had ignited a spark of discourse, opinions divided and perspectives wildly divergent.

A group at a nearby table chimed in, their conversation merging with the growing buzz of uncertainty. "I know it's complex, but what about the people there, the ones who've been working with us? What's going to happen to them?" One airman was leaning back, rocking his chair on its legs, trying to see how far his opinion would reach.

It reached far enough, a reply coming, saying, "It's a mess, no doubt about that. But sometimes, there are no easy answers. Just because we want to find one doesn't mean it's there."

From a different corner of the mess hall, a seasoned airman added, "Think about the resources, the years of effort we've poured into this. Feels like it's all going down the drain."

A young female airman joined in. "What about the peace we were trying to bring? All those discussions, negotiations, sacrifices." Her voice betrayed a mountain of frustration.

Against this backdrop, I stood amidst the ebb and flow, a witness to the collective response to this seismic revelation. Friends approached, seeking solace in shared uncertainty, while others sought guidance from me as if I held the key to understanding this tumultuous twist of fate. But as all the multitude of voices swirled, converging and separating, a growing sense of overwhelm was tugging at my thoughts. The heaviness of the moment, the magnitude of the decision, all these diverse elements came crashing upon me like an unrelenting wave. With a sudden resolve, I excused myself, leaving my untouched breakfast and a mug of steaming tea behind.

I swiftly made my way to my office.

The walk back to my safe harbor seemed so long, yet it was barely a few corridors before I was back in my own space. And there, behind the swiftly closed door, I allowed myself the briefest moment to catch my breath, running a hand across my hair. The scene outside felt distant now, as if already processed and filtered through a fine-meshed veil of disbelief. I sank into my chair, trying to process it all.

The delicate equilibrium of hope and reality had just been shattered, and the road ahead had metamorphosed into some uncertain, stony, unmade path, obscured by the dust of my crumbling aspirations. And amid this turbulent set of feelings, the boundaries between reality and the haunting specter of yesterday's stress only seemed to blur into one another.

However, any lingering delusion was promptly dispelled, the urgent intrusion of Sergeant Garcia disrupting my thoughts. He was not a figment of my mind but right there, standing before my desk, tapping his fingers on the desktop as if impatient. But I took it as a minor sign of slight frustration at the news that had just made its way to accost us all.

Before a single word could escape his lips, my thoughts erupted into an urgent torrent, spilling forth in a desperate bid for some semblance of clarity and relief.

"How's the situation out there?" I asked, my voice showing concern and curiosity. "Such a mess, isn't it?"

"Considering how everyone's just found out, it's somewhat chaotic but entirely as expected," he voiced and leaned forward, his expression pensive and his tone a touch subdued. "Opinions and beliefs are being voiced left and right. But you know, they just need time to process everything; it will all be *business as usual* again before we know it. Anyway, how are you holding up?"

"I don't know. I'm just worried, I guess," I confessed, my words giving away the kind of hint of vulnerability I hated to show.

He picked up on my discomfort.

"Worrying is natural in times like these," he announced, his voice offering me a calm reassurance, yet within me, a storm continued to rage unchecked against my meek façade.

Amidst the tide of racing thoughts, I pressed on. "I'm just trying to wrap my head around the sheer magnitude of it all. Deploying pilots, organizing search and retrieval teams, it's overwhelming. The influx of fleets adds to the complexity. Time's clearly of the essence."

He nodded; his manner composed. "First, let's take a deep breath." He had picked up on the tremor of fractiousness and the slight way my utterance grew too breathy at the end.

But as my mind raced, a desperate urge to convey urgency was still gnawing away at me.

His soft invocation of my name brought a momentary pause, a gentle plea briefly quieting the storm within for a second time. "Captain," he said, his voice a quiet yet commanding reassurance that anchored me to the present. "Please, take a breath. Try not to let it rattle you."

Compliant, I drew in a slow, steadying breath, a conscious effort to quell the tumultuous tide of my thoughts. He followed soothingly with, "The situation's being managed. While you do have a pivotal role to play, there's no need to bear the gravitas of it all alone. Allow yourself some respite from the strain. You have a good team to assist you, and they'll step up."

As understanding settled in, I nodded in a gesture of gratitude mingled with a newfound semblance of calm. But a semblance was all it was, my guts roiling.

"All we know as of now is that we are leaving, Captain," he stated. "There have been no other specified or official orders as yet. The announcement has not been followed through with a plan. Maybe they are waiting on other intel to move forward with the evacuation."

"Okay, so we are currently at the initial stage of the retreat, yes?"

His nod confirmed my understanding. "As for the plan," he prompted, his tone inviting me to speak what I thought ought to happen now.

I leaned in, a bit uncertain. "Following the evacuation announcement, the base will naturally call upon every aircraft in the Air Force fleet. We'll need all hands-on deck, a coordinated effort to manage the increased air traffic, radio and communication demands."

He nodded thoughtfully, interjecting with measured wisdom, "Air traffic management is a given that will already be managed, but the workload will surge."

"Then there are the new airmen arriving," I continued, musing aloud. "Sorting them into teams or consolidating them into existing ones. It's a decision calling for clarity."

"The latter might be more practical," he suggested. "Establishing new teams could strain resources and coordination. I'd say to utilize the existing structure to maximize efficiency. Creating a new team would be too great a hassle to manage in a situation like this."

I nodded. "I'll discuss this with Lieutenant Colonel Peterson. Aligning with the chain of command's going to be crucial at this juncture."

"Absolutely," he affirmed, his confidence reinforcing my resolve. "And what about the team management?"

"We'll adhere to protocol and communicate the news, no sugar coating anything. Transparency is key," I asserted.

He nodded in agreement. "Remember, though...again, you have a team for a reason. They'll rely on your leadership, and you on theirs. Don't try to deal with things alone."

We left the office and parted ways, my steps determined, albeit bowed by the weight of what I had taken upon myself. I traversed the corridor toward Lieutenant Colonel Peterson's office, my mind consumed by the impending discussion before I halted right by his door, taking a moment to collect my thoughts before knocking and entering.

"Ah, Captain Katz. I assume you have heard the announcement," Lieutenant Colonel Peterson acknowledged as he opened up the door to me, his tone measured and way too calm by my reckoning—though of course, he wouldn't ever present himself any other way.

"Yes, sir. And I would like to discuss our approach moving forward." I wanted to keep my demeanor professional, putting effort into my voice staying steady and unflustered. Another show of emotion was not something I would tolerate in myself at this time. That breathiness at the end of my sentences had to be overcome too, something I had to work on improving.

He gestured for me to sit; his eyes fixed on mine. "Please, go ahead."

"Sir, the paucity of information concerns me. I believe sharing any available intel would aid our preparations," I implored.

He exhaled, breath laden with the weight of reality. "I understand your concern, Captain. But that's all we have, an order we have to follow. The verdict is final. We will be retreating."

"I understand, but I just don't want to step onto the field blind, sir," I reasoned.

"And you will not. We have all our resources pooling in from everywhere—more men, more fleets—all to aid in this operation. We are all here to help," he assured.

I shifted in my seat, my discomfort evident. "But sir, there's more to consider—humanitarian issues, security risks. The refugees, the turmoil that may follow."

"Indeed," he conceded, his expression grave. "Our duty is twofold, to withdraw our forces and address the consequences. Your role in this is vital, Captain."

My mind raced, stress and pressure forcing in from all sides. My lips pursed as if they had a mind of their own, but I was thinking of what to say, floundering for statements that would not render me sounding even more desperate to a man so unbearably cool and collected.

"Can I trust you to play your part, to execute the operation dutifully?" he queried, his eyes piercing, not interested in waiting for my next set of uncertainties.

I hesitated again though, my heart drumming. "Yes, sir," I affirmed somehow, trepidation and a dearth of certainty almost surely in my voice.

"Good," he stated, a nod sealing our pact.

Back in my office, the enormity of the challenge remained. Saying *yes, sir* was one thing. Delivering on the situation and—to me—cataclysmic promise was quite another, and I had not yet fathomed the means of achieving what he had asked for. But soon, I would have to address my team, to share the burden of understanding, offering a glimmer of hope.

I strived to exude stability, yet my thoughts were a tempest seeking a steady anchor, tossed this way and that. It wasn't just my footing I sought; it was stability for all those depending on me.

The afternoon stretched out before me, an expanse of time to weave my thoughts and craft my words. Anticipation threatened to swallow me whole like Jonah inside the whale at the harrowing anticipation of my first official meeting with the team to address the current situation. Anxious energy coursed through me; their minds were likely abuzz with questions, and it fell to me to provide the answers. Ones I presently did not have.

Early in my journey, I had gleaned the art of strategic omission, a skill distinct from lying. It was a means to delicately veil the truth for the sake of order. Through military conferences and practiced smiles, I had learned to project an air of confidence even in moments of grave self-doubt. It was a means to instill calm in times of marked unease, to lead with apparent assurance.

Summoning Sergeant Garcia, I learned that the team had assembled in the meeting room. Shortly, I headed there too, but my old friend anxiety was grabbing me around the throat, threatening to throttle me before I'd begin to play my part. Akin to a vile demon perched on my shoulder, it was now leaning in and whispering at the edges of my composure, bringing palpitations and dampening my palms with nervous energy.

I stifled the unease, acutely aware that no one in my team could witness me faltering in front of them. Surreptitiously, I wiped my hands on my thighs, then shoved wide the double doors.

Walking into the room, I faced a sea of expectant faces. We exchanged pleasantries, introductions, and nods of camaraderie before delving right away into the very heart of the matter. I outlined the knowledge gleaned from Lieutenant Colonel Peterson and the insights gathered from conversations with John. My voice was going to waver soon enough, and I knew it ahead of time, telling myself it would be only slightly as I'd explain how we would proceed, adhering to protocol during this initial stage. Hopefully, only I would be conscious of the nasty cold sweat sliding down into the small of my back, wetting the fabric of my clothes, making them cling.

"Thank you all for gathering here," I began, my gaze sweeping the room. "I want to provide you with a clear understanding of our current situation and the steps we'll be taking moving forward. As you know, the recent announcement has brought about significant changes, and it's crucial we work together to navigate through this challenge."

A hand shot up, and I nodded. "Yes, Airman Harris?"

"Captain, do we have any further intel on the situation? Any specific details about the evacuation that we should be aware of?"

An excellent question, one highlighting the need for more information. "Thank you for bringing that up, Airman. At this stage, we have received initial directives regarding the evacuation. Our priority is to ensure our readiness to respond effectively. As we receive additional intel, we'll adapt our approach accordingly."

Another voice chimed in, that of Airman Martinez. "Captain Katz, considering the complexity of the situation, how are we to navigate through? What strategies will we employ to ensure our team's effectiveness?"

"Navigating this challenge will require a multifaceted approach, but our initial focus will be on reinforcing our communication networks, ensuring our resources are optimized, and maintaining readiness for potential shifts. As we move forward, our strategies will be built upon the foundation of coordination, adaptability, and a shared commitment to our mission."

A sense of determination radiated from the group, but I felt sure of detecting more than a scattering of underlying concerns. Trying to move swiftly past these issues would not benefit anyone, so I took a deep breath before clarifying, "I want to create an environment of open discussion. Your questions and insights are invaluable. Let's address any uncertainties you have."

Airman Jackson cleared his throat. "Captain, what about the potential influx of refugees? How are we preparing for that scenario, and how does it factor into our plans?"

"A valid point, Airman Jackson. While we don't have precise details about this as yet, we must be prepared to support humanitarian efforts. Our team's resources and expertise will play a role in this aspect as well. As we gather more information, we'll collaborate with relevant parties to ensure a coordinated response."

"Captain Katz," Airman Phillips called out. "Given the potential increase in activity, how do we ensure efficient coordination with other teams on the base?"

"Collaboration will indeed be vital, and our collective goal is to ensure seamless coordination and a cohesive effort that contributes to the overall mission."

As the discussion continued, more questions arose, each a testament to the dedication and recognition of the personnel's responsibility. I addressed their concerns, guided by a desire to provide clarity and instill confidence. In that room, I was seeing not just a team, but a collection of individuals united by purpose, determined to rise above all challenges.

"Our mission is significant, and I have faith in each of you," I concluded. "We're a cohesive force, ready to confront the unknown. The path ahead may be complex, but together, we have the strength to navigate it."

My words issued a defiant proclamation of our shared purpose.

I met the gazes of fellow airmen, glimpsing the fire of determination blazing within them too. Uncertainty may have lain ahead, but fueled by our united sense of purpose, we stood ready to confront whatever challenges loomed.

Swift with my return to my office, I was soon brimming with joy due to the successful meeting. And just when I thought the day had reached its peak, a pleasantly surprising turn of events transpired: Captain Solomon made an entrance.

"Hey," I blurted out, realizing I'd been holding my anticipation in check for too long.

"Hi, are you busy with something?" Brian's voice held a calm and composed quality, a reflection of the person he was.

I replied a touch too hastily, "No, not at the moment. Nothing pressing, at least. Everything all right?"

"I just landed and finished my mission debrief. I figured I'd stop by. So, here's the proposition: would you be interested in watching a movie with me?"

For a brief moment, I stood frozen, caught off guard by the unexpected invitation.

He continued, "I thought it would be good to loosen up. It's not a grand affair, just a modest laptop screen in the back of my truck. I trust that will meet with your approval?"

The silence kept building tension until I finally replied with sincerity, "I would love to watch a movie with you. And the simplicity is perfectly fine!"

A radiant smile broke across his face, relief and delight evident. "Great," he affirmed, his demeanor exuding confidence tempered with gentle humility.

Strolling along the fringes of the base, our steps unhurried, we shared a companionable silence that felt remarkably comfortable. In contrast to my previous notions, this silence didn't bear the discomfort or emptiness of before. Walking alongside Captain Solomon, I found myself immersed in a unique blend of awe and ease. He held an undeniable refinement about him, a presence exuding power and resilience. But I had decided the name "Brian" was almost insufficient to denote all this. I would henceforth think of him as Captain Solomon.

Lost in my musings, he startled me when he said, "Here we are." His gesture directed my attention toward a sizable truck, conspicuously elevated and equipped with formidable wheels, a clear testament to its military-grade stature.

Brian deftly hopped into the back before extending a hand to assist me, and as I clambered up, a fleeting stumble leading me to momentarily collide with his chest. A mutual blush stained our cheeks, a subtle moment of shared embarrassment that we tactfully disregarded.

Regaining my composure, I inadvertently brushed against an object, something that emitted a faint crinkling noise. "Oh," I uttered softly, my fingers exploring the source of the unexpected sensation, revealing a trove of snacks nestled within a door pocket.

A sheepish smile graced Brian's lips, bashful. "Ah, I managed to gather a few bits and pieces to nibble. No movie night can be considered complete without popcorn, right?"

"So, this stuff is popcorn?" I asked, unable to see since my eyes hadn't adjusted yet.

"No, not popcorn, unfortunately." He giggled and I joined in. "It's the next best thing. Chocolate, nuts…"

I giggled again, more heartily. "So, you invited me here only to have no popcorn? I feel misled, hoodwinked…"

"Believe me, I'm sorry. But I took quite a few friendly bets with fellow airmen to amass this stash," he said. "I figured you might enjoy them anyway."

"We might enjoy them," I corrected, grinning.

"No, no *we*. I got them just for you," he said. His hand scratched the back of his head, a gesture that revealed a charming vulnerability, a glimpse into the softer side of his confident exterior.

"I must say, a man who comes prepared is quite impressive," I remarked with a note of genuine appreciation.

It was his turn to grin, exuding satisfaction and playfulness. "It does feel pretty good to be that guy." But he really was prepared.

The truck's interior had been transformed into a cozy haven, the floor covered in soft blankets and spare pillows likely sourced from his personal quarters or borrowed from his comrades. A makeshift table elevated the laptop to eye level, flanked by an array of snacks and drinks, all curated to align with my preferences. Brian's keen attention to detail didn't escape my notice.

As the movie began, I harbored no lofty expectations for the cinematic experience; besides, the film was a romance, a safe and predictable choice.

Capturing my blank stare, Brian took the initiative to verbalize his thoughts. Leaning in slightly, his voice took on a gentle inflection. "You know, there's a subtle charm to this movie."

A playful retort escaped me, a teasing smile accompanying my words. "Don't give away spoilers now. Or wait...you don't even have to."

His smile widened, a gleam of amusement in his eyes. "So, you're implying you've seen it before?"

"No, but I can predict the ending. I'm fairly certain they'll end up falling in love," I remarked, my gaze drifting to the characters on the screen. "Kind of predictable, huh?"

A moment of silence ensued before he resumed, his tone contemplative. "And you reckon that's all there is to it. But there's so much more to unravel."

Curious, I turned to fully face him. "Such as?"

"Like those subtle gestures that convey volumes without a single word, the eyes that mirror a love transcending language. The journey of falling, it's a tapestry woven with intricate threads," he explained. As his words flowed, an inexplicable intensity emanated from his gaze, momentarily challenging my ability to meet his eyes.

His insight lingered, and for a heartbeat, I found it hard to avert my gaze. His perspective had unveiled a layer of depth, transforming the movie into a metaphor for all the myriad complexities of human connection. It was a revelation that left behind a lingering resonance, one that had lifted from the silver screen and now was sounding between us.

The movie soon faded into the background, overshadowed by the profound awareness of Brian's proximity. Our closeness was palpable, his hands occasionally brushing against mine before swiftly retreating, a subtle dance of contact and withdrawal. I couldn't help but note his own consciousness of our physical proximity, mirrored in the fleeting touches and the way his gaze occasionally wandered toward me.

And he whispered my name oh so gently. "Norah."

The movie's narrative swiftly became secondary, a mere murmur in the backdrop of shared moments. Instead, the intensity of our mutual regard took center stage, an invisible thread weaving between us, escaping the confines of the laptop, enveloping us in its own narrative.

Our bodies leaned into each other's embrace, a magnetic pull holding us just a hair's breadth apart. His fingertips grazed mine in a delicate dance, igniting a cascade of tingling sensations that rippled through my senses. In that charged moment, my mind hummed with a potent blend of longing and excitement, each heartbeat echoing with anticipation.

"I don't mean to be forward," Brian said, voice quivering slightly, his gaze locking onto mine.

A surge of warmth coursed through me as his hand cupped the side of my face, his touch inviting and reassuring. Yielding to the instinctual pull, I leaned into the caress, savoring the tenderness of his gesture. His demeanor shifted, a telltale sign of what really swirled beneath the surface. A palpable tension clung to us, mingling with the cadence of his heavier breaths. His eyes, like windows to his soul, held an unspoken yearning—a plea venturing beyond words, beyond the realm of my comprehension.

Before he could give voice to his unspoken thoughts, a whisper escaped my lips, carrying an unexpected, "Yes." The syllable hung in stillness, a vulnerable admission that I scarcely understood myself. At that moment, I did not care what I had agreed to. It didn't even matter.

His surprise mirrored my own, a flicker of astonishment dancing across his features. Seizing the possibility, I leaned forward, bridging the scant distance separating us. Our lips met with a hesitating tenderness, a gentle melding that encapsulated the innocence of shared vulnerability.

It was a kiss painted with delicate strokes of curiosity, evoking the flutter of a newfound emotion, a delicate bloom in the garden of our connection.

The sensations—the soft brush of his skin, the faint racing of my heart—etched themselves into my memory, a cherished testament to our beautiful and unscripted encounter.

As we eventually drew apart, I could imagine the air shimmering with unspoken revelations. A mix of wonder and realization lingered in the softness of his gaze, a silent understanding to affirm the tender intimacy we'd just shared. It was a kiss that spoke of beginnings, a charming prologue to a story yet to be written, innocent and sweet in its unfolding.

Refuge amidst Chaos

In the days following the initial news, the base buzzed with frantic energy, a hive of constant movement. The once expansive spaces seemed to shrink as the influx of personnel created a newfound sense of bustling activity. The symphony of engine noises, the rhythmic dance of planes landing and taking off, all grew stronger as a harmoniously thrumming backdrop.

To me, these sounds were familiar, a reminder of my role as an airman, a comforting contrast to the sterile silence of paperwork-laden rooms holding no allure for me.

As time passed, the initial shock of the tidings began to settle, allowing a semblance of normalcy to return. However, this "normal" was a new shade, daubed with the brushstrokes of change. The base, once a well-known backdrop, now wore an altered face. The pace of life had quickened, driven by the hum of machinery and the shuffling of feet.

Yet amid the flurry of activity, a quiet transformation was unfolding. The calm after the initial storm brought with it an uptick in administrative duties. Paperwork was becoming an omnipresent companion, constantly multiplying. The expanding ranks and growing fleet demanded meticulous record-keeping, something that fell upon each of us.

In parallel, the conference rooms came alive with many voices, where once only the rustle of paper had been heard. Team meetings became the arena for forging alliances, collaboration becoming imperative. The newcomers, fresh faces in this evolving landscape, found themselves enveloped in a deluge of debriefings, each exchange contributing to the seamless integration of new and old.

It felt like an ordinary day as I stood outside Lieutenant Colonel Peterson's office, his summons echoing a routine update in my mind. I anticipated discussing the base's progress and the smoothness of our operations. Armed with revised words and concise information, I entered, ready to present my report. Yet the atmosphere in the office bore an undercurrent of tension, a telltale sign of something greatly amiss. I should have recognized the cues, the furrowed brow and intensity of his gaze, indicators of impending news that would shatter the ground beneath my feet.

As I settled into the chair across from Lieutenant Colonel Peterson, an uncharacteristic stress showed in his expression. A pang of apprehension triggered in me, a prelude to the storm about to engulf my world. His words, when they came, crashed over me like a tidal wave. "I wish it were under better circumstances, but I must share something of the utmost importance."

My instincts sharpened, and a sense of foreboding rushed in. "What is it, sir?"

He took a deep breath, his words betraying knowledge of a world in turmoil. "Bagram has fallen. Less than twenty-four hours since we withdrew our forces, the Taliban have recaptured the territory."

My spirits plummeted.

He continued, "The U.S. military now only holds the Hamid Karzai International Airport, where all the refugees have been gathered. The urgency has intensified. We have about forty-eight hours to evacuate approximately 150,000 Afghan refugees."

My voice was a mere whisper, partially disabled by realization. "The scale of this...it's overwhelming, sir."

Lieutenant Colonel Peterson's gaze met mine, the gravity of the situation mirrored in his eyes. "That's why I have called you in, Captain. We need all hands-on deck for a large-scale rescue operation. All available C-17s will be mobilized, and our foreign partners are joining the effort with their cargo planes."

I absorbed all that I could. "What can I do to assist, sir?"

Lieutenant Colonel Peterson's voice held a blend of urgency and resolve. "Your leadership, Captain. Your skills and guidance are going to be crucial in ensuring the success of this mission. The world's largest airlift operation will commence in forty-eight hours."

Leaving Lieutenant Colonel Peterson's office, a surge of intent coursed through me, overpowering any doubt or hesitation. Time was a luxury we could not afford to squander, and as the leader of my team, I had to marshal our efforts swiftly and decisively.

Gathering every piece of information available, I meticulously assembled a comprehensive situational overview. Once I had scrutinized and confirmed everything in my own mind, I embarked on the task of formulating a plan. But my mind was awash with possibilities, each one needing to be dissected, evaluated, and considered against the fragile circumstances in which we found ourselves. Doubts and second-guesses were peppering my thoughts. A plan that wasn't foolproof simply wouldn't suffice; there was no room for errors.

I contacted Sergeant Garcia, who swiftly mobilized the team, his efficiency a reflection of the urgency. Within a conference room, I stepped in to speak, feeling how the situation would demand everything from me. The atmosphere here was charged.

"Thank you all for coming here," I began. "We are facing an unprecedented challenge, and I have no doubt that each of you is up to the task."

Sergeant Garcia spoke up, leaning forward, looking me squarely in the eyes. "Captain, what's the plan?"

"Our mission is clear. Our immediate focus is on coordinating the evacuation of refugees from Hamid Karzai International Airport. We need to ensure seamless communication and collaboration with our foreign partners, who are sending their cargo planes to assist."

A chorus of steadfast agreements rippled across the room, eyes locking onto mine. Ideas ignited and discussions flowed as we forged ahead, outlining strategies, dissecting potential contingencies, and evaluating the resources at our disposal. The room hummed with a blend of energy and focus, each member contributing their expertise to shape the course of action that would define our mission.

Lost in thought, I strode down the corridor on my way to my office after the team meeting, my mind still caught in a tsunami of tasks and plans. Mentally rehearsing my forthcoming meeting with Lieutenant Colonel and the section chiefs, I refined my responses, ensuring every detail stayed in my memory. This meeting, a collective effort to ensure our objectives and plans were harmonized, aimed at fostering cohesion and aligning strategies.

My preoccupied state had somehow rendered me deaf to the impatient calling of my name until a hand gently stopped me from opening the office door. It broke me out of my trance, my eyes shifting from the door handle to the face before me. I turned my head around to see Captain Solomon. He looked at me with concern, then guided us both into my office, discreetly closing the door behind him and leaning against it.

He crossed his arms. "I called out to you twice, Captain." His voice betrayed a tone of worry.

"I apologize," I responded, embarrassed. "My thoughts were running rampant."

His arms crossed, Captain Solomon took a few steps closer, his gaze locked on mine. "Is everything all right?"

I sighed, his concern suddenly growing too oppressive for me. "Just the upcoming meeting. This situation has everyone on edge."

His eyes studied my face, a silent understanding passing between us. Then, in a surprising move, he closed the distance to wrap me in a soft embrace. Startled, I quickly found solace in his hug, a sense of comfort washing over me.

"You're all right though?" he inquired, his breath brushing against my ear.

"Yes," I murmured, my voice muffled by his shoulder. "Just a lot to handle, that's all."

He pulled back slightly, eyeing me again. "I understand. Listen, I have my first flight out tomorrow morning and a debrief meeting scheduled a few minutes from now, amidst all this melee. But I was hoping we could grab dinner tonight, before I leave."

A small smile tugged at my lips, grateful for the respite his offer promised. "Sure."

In response, Captain Solomon's gaze seemed to soften even further, his fingers lightly tracing the curve of my hand before he gently lifted it to his lips. His breath was a delicate caress against my skin as he pressed a tender kiss to my forehead, a gesture that held a silent promise. His reassurance was welcomed.

"Take care of yourself, okay?" he murmured, his voice carrying sincerity.

I nodded, a sigh escaping as a warmth spread through me, like sunlight breaking through clouds. "You, too."

With that, he left, his presence remaining, akin to a delicate echo. The touch of his lips stayed on my forehead, a sweet reminder amidst too many things to get done. As I returned to my preparations, I held onto that fleeting moment, a cherished pause.

Of course, it could not stay that way, and it wasn't long before the urgency of the situation propelled me toward the conference room. My steps quickened, a tangible sense of purpose pushing me forward. With a timely arrival, I took my seat among a gathering of section chiefs and Lieutenant Colonel Peterson, the atmosphere burdened by formality and grave faces.

"Let's commence," Lieutenant Colonel Peterson said, setting the tone. The room itself seemed to hold its breath, awaiting the comprehensive overview about to unfold.

Radio Section Chief, Staff Sergeant Chacon, the expert in radio operations, spoke up first. "Our communication channels with foreign partners are active and constant, and their cargo planes are scheduled to arrive in staggered waves over the next twenty-four hours. We have coordinated the air traffic and fine-tuned radio operations to manage the anticipated influx seamlessly."

Technical Sergeant James, Server Section Chief, followed up. "We are focusing on resource management as a critical priority. Protocols are being implemented to optimize data exchange and maintain peak server performance."

My turn came, and I outlined our team's strategy, emphasizing collaboration with refugees on the ground. "We are working on establishing strategic communication hubs at the airport, categorizing refugees, and streamlining the boarding process for maximum efficiency."

Leaning forward, Lieutenant Colonel Peterson introduced the man beside him. "This is Master Sergeant Ramirez, who will be providing us with the latest intelligence updates from Afghanistan." He then turned to him, posing a question. "Are there any developments we need to be aware of?"

Intelligence Section Chief Ramirez provided a composed response.

"We are closely monitoring the situation on the ground. At the moment, there have been no significant escalations. We are maintaining a vigilant stance."

Another voice spoke up from around the table. "Our foreign partners' support is of paramount importance. What's the status of their aid?" It was Supply Section Chief Johnson.

Lieutenant Colonel Peterson's answer gave some slight assurance. "Medical supplies, food, and essential resources are enroute. The initial wave of cargo planes from our partners is set to touch down within the next twelve hours."

The conversation flowed seamlessly, a symphony of voices harmonizing in the face of a complex challenge. As the group exchanged information, addressed concerns, and proposed solutions, a sense of unity emerged, woven into each spoken word.

In this room, among the uncertainty, we found a steady anchor. Our collective expertise, dedication, and firm resolve to get the job done would be the bedrock upon which this audacious rescue operation stood. Every sentence uttered, every decision made, reinforced the resilience uniting us in the pursuit of a shared mission—one that transcended borders and illustrated the boundless strength of human resolve when faced with adversity.

The ongoing mission demands, combined with an unrelenting sense of responsibility, were all beginning to chip away at my resolve. There was a lurking fear, an unsettling doubt, gnawing at me from within. It was a fear that my carefully crafted strategy could falter, that I could fail not just my team, but also the entire base.

As I sat in that room surrounded by faces exuding confidence and expertise, a sense of inadequacy settled in. These were professionals, masters of their respective domains, and here I was, struggling to convince myself that I belonged amongst them. I felt like an imposter, an outsider playing a role in a world of power that I was not entirely sure I could wield.

Amid the sea of paperwork that consumed my desk, a faint chime from my phone beckoned for attention. I reached for it, a spark of curiosity kindling within me as I glimpsed Captain Solomon's name on the screen. Yet, as his message unfolded, a bittersweet sigh escaped.

His words conveyed regret, a gentle apology for missing our planned dinner. Strangely, I found myself unable to summon any hint of frustration or annoyance. How could I, when our shared responsibilities bore down upon us? Our relationship, a fragile ember amidst the raging inferno of our duties, often found itself playing second fiddle to work commitments. Besides, the fact that his presence within the base was as transient as the wind did little to soothe my heart.

A melancholic undertow pulled at me as I pondered the intricacies of our connection. The nature of my emotions was as elusive as the wisps of smoke, difficult to grasp, yet casting a long shadow of doubt upon the canvas of our love. In these turbulent times, hope seemed to wither like a fragile flower, despite my fervent desire for it to flourish.

Sadness was settling in, though I chose to ward it off by extending my working hours into the night. The soft glow of my desk lamp illuminated the files scattered before me, like a pool of knowledge waiting to be explored. I lost myself in the task, sorting through papers and absorbing every memo to stay updated on the evolving situation.

Outside, the base was enshrouded in a soothing hush, a rare moment of tranquility. With each document I pursued, I could sense the puzzle pieces of the operation fitting together, forming a clearer picture of our mission's intricacies.

Sergeant Garcia's message blinked on my screen, hinting at a potential meeting involving key officers, including Lieutenant Colonels Peterson, Williams, Adams and Evans. While it wasn't confirmed yet, the idea of their arrival underscored the importance of effective communication and strategy alignment. The prospect of a collaborative session also loomed, urging me to prepare for the possibility.

As the night deepened, I embraced the solitude and the rhythmic scratch of my pen against paper. The impending meeting added a layer of anticipation to my vigil, and I delved into my work with a renewed sense of purpose. In this quiet space, I found solace and a way to push back the profound depression that had threatened to take hold.

That was until Captain Solomon's unexpected entrance into my office jolted me from my word-induced trance. His surprise mirrored my own, as if he had not expected to see anyone here. It didn't matter though, because there he was, a tangible presence that made my heart race.

"Sorry about barging in," he said, regaining his composure. "I saw the lights on; I just thought that you might have forgotten to turn them off."

"Oh," was all that I could manage, still processing his sudden appearance. "No problem at all," I then replied quickly, pushing aside the files over which I had been poring.

He walked closer, closing the gap between us. His hands gently reached forward to hold mine. "Well, perhaps our meeting is serendipitous," he ventured. "Either way, I'm glad I could see you before I leave in the morning."

His words stirred a mix of longing and conflict in my chest. Our duties always took precedence, but it was the moments like these that made it challenging.

I couldn't feel selfish when it came to him, yet unbeknownst to me, tears welled up, a silent testament to the turmoil roiling in me. He reached out, his thumb brushing away a stray tear, every sinew of me aching at the tenderness in his gesture.

"What's wrong? Why are you crying?"

I hesitated, grappling with unchecked stirrings. "Because I feel torn," I confessed, my voice trembling with vulnerability.

His eyes looked so dejected. He cupped my cheeks, his eyes locking onto mine in a reassuring gaze. "I wish I could stay longer," he admitted, a tone of regret in his voice.

But he couldn't have stayed, even if I had asked him to.

I nodded, understanding but so sad. "I know," I whispered, my fingers instinctively reaching to touch his hand.

Leaning in, he pressed his lips against mine in a tender, lingering kiss, a bittersweet mixture of comfort and farewell. "Take care of yourself."

As he turned to leave, all my inner sentiments seemed at odds as I watched him go, my heart torn between the desire to hold onto him and the understanding that called to me. With a deep sigh, I also decided to return to my tent, the memory of his kiss still strong. Despite the melancholic tendrils that sought to ensnare me, I found the strength to tuck those feelings away, hoping to sleep. Closing my eyes, the darkness was invited to enfold me, delivering me safely to a sanctuary in which worries and uncertainties could find temporary respite.

The shrill sound of an emergency alert pierced the stillness of my room, instantly snapping me out of slumber. Anxiety curdled my stomach as I fumbled to grab my phone, the glowing screen revealing a message needing no further explanation. Urgent and significant developments had arisen, demanding immediate attention.

Without hesitation, I quickly donned my uniform, the fabric a familiar second skin carrying with it a sense of purpose and duty.

As I stepped out, my gaze met Master Sergeant Garcia's, a silent understanding passing between us. Neither of us speaking, we made eye contact and acknowledged the seriousness of the situation, then with one nod of agreement, we set off together toward our designated meeting location. Today marked the commencement of the daunting rescue mission, a colossal effort to evacuate the Afghan refugees. The mood was charged with tension.

Sergeant Garcia's voice cut through the hurried buzz of activity. "We've got an urgent meeting. Lieutenant Colonel Adams wants everyone together."

I nodded briskly, my mind already shifting gears as I joined Sergeant Garcia on the path to the meeting room. Anticipation was mingling with our collective purpose.

As I entered the room, the atmosphere seemed to thicken. The gathered leadership—Lieutenant Colonel Peterson, Lieutenant Colonel Williams, Lieutenant Colonel Adams, and Lieutenant Colonel Evans—stood united, a formidable front prepared to confront the full spectrum of challenges that lay ahead.

General Davidson, the wing commander, took the floor with a presence demanding attention. Fatigue had furrowed lines on his face, a testament to how serious the situation was.

His words were deliberate and clear, outlining the urgency and magnitude of the mission. Our C-17s were allocated to Central Command for the Afghan refugee evacuation, and Al Udeid Air Base had been tasked with a vital role in providing shelter and aid to a significant portion of those displaced.

A somber hush settled over the room as he spoke with a commanding air. I exchanged a fleeting look with Lieutenant Colonel Peterson, the unspoken understanding between us mirroring the enormity of everything now resting on our shoulders. The room seemed to pulse with a collective acknowledgment that this endeavor would require our utmost dedication.

The discussion unfolded, punctuated by tense exchanges and urgent inquiries, our dialogue reflecting how great was the magnitude of the challenges we faced. Lieutenant Colonel Williams' voice held an edge of urgency as she voiced concerns about logistical hurdles, while Lieutenant Colonel Evans' measured input highlighted the need for efficient communication channels.

Amidst the intense deliberations, Lieutenant Colonel Peterson leaned in, his words directed to me in a quiet undertone. "Pay attention, Captain. This is where it all comes together."

His guidance was spurring me to focus even more keenly on the dialogue, every commander in the room invested in this shared mission, unwilling to be distracted from dissecting of each facet of the operation.

Lieutenant Colonel Adams turned to me, his gaze intense. "Captain, how prepared is your team for the influx of refugees?"

I met his gaze directly. "We've been working round the clock to set up communication hubs and ensure efficient boarding procedures. Our team is ready, sir."

The room seemed to collectively hold its breath on the precipice of a monumental undertaking, and the coming days would test our mettle in ways we could scarcely imagine. Yet amidst the tension, a unity of purpose forged a bond between us all, a shared commitment to alleviate suffering and make a difference.

As the meeting drew to a close, I exchanged a nod with Lieutenant Colonel Peterson, a silent affirmation. The room emptied, everyone alert to the unmissable awareness of all we needed to accomplish. Lieutenant Colonel Peterson's guidance swathed me like a blanket, and with his support and the joint strength of the team, we would navigate the challenges and bring hope to those in dire need.

The mission was under way.

Master Sergeant Garcia and I regrouped with the section chiefs, united, understanding the urgency of the situation and the roles we each played in it. Addressing them, I acknowledged the challenges while stressing strategic resource allocation.

One of them raised a concern about potential exhaustion among their teams.

I would prioritize the men's well-being, I reassured him, while still pushing for maximum effort to meet the mission's demands.

"We have an opportunity to make a significant impact here," Master Sergeant Garcia interjected, his voice firm with conviction. "The refugees and aircrews are counting on us, and we can't let them down." It was a passionate reminder of the mission's importance.

Brainstorming began for resource allocation and installation plans. We decided to utilize existing equipment, including around four hundred un-imaged computers and forty phones kept in storage for future projects. The team nodded in agreement. We all knew that this was just the beginning, many challenges waiting for us ahead, but we were prepared to do whatever it took to make this mission successful.

Back in my office, what it meant to be flight commander was all too apparent, especially given recent events. It was a grievous sense of obligation, now threatening to overwhelm me. I inhaled deeply, attempting to regain my composure, yet the thoughts were refusing to clear. Doubts clouded my mind; I worried about making the right decisions for my team and for all those who were looking to me for their continued guidance and safety.

In a rare moment of vulnerability, I offered a silent prayer, seeking guidance and the strength to persevere, refusing to let apprehension and uncertainty hold me back.

My phone's urgent ring echoed on the desk, the classified line lighting up. It was Lieutenant Colonel Peterson, and instinctively, I knew this call wouldn't bring good news.

"Captain Katz…" His voice was steady but serious as I answered. "We've got updates on the mission commander requirements."

Listening intently, my mind raced, absorbing the implications of his words. The numbers he mentioned hit me like a shockwave—fifty C-17s and forty-five C-130s, a significant increase from our original plan and a challenge we hadn't fully anticipated.

I discussed potential solutions with him, but it became clear that we needed more equipment, an extra five hundred computers and fifty secure phones, a daunting task, particularly considering our tight resources.

With Lieutenant Colonel Peterson's nod of approval, we decided to repurpose resources from lower-priority sites. It wasn't ideal but was our best shot, given the time crunch. We had just twenty-four hours to execute this plan and get everything ready for the influx.

As I hung up, my heart felt downbeat, this new task threatening to stretch my team beyond its limits. I had to voice my concerns.

"Sir, do we have any additional support coming in?" My voice trembled slightly as I asked, hoping for him to cast me a lifeline.

He responded bluntly, "No, we're on our own. Passenger movements are halted across the area."

The realization hit me like a punch to the gut. We were in uncharted territory, facing an uphill battle with no reinforcements. I clenched my fists, my freshly trimmed and scrubbed fingernails almost embedding into my clammy palms.

"Captain, this is where the rubber meets the road." Lieutenant Colonel Peterson's words were somehow both reassuring and challenging. At least he had made it clear where we stood. "We're pushing beyond normal, Captain, but the team is capable."

There was a heady interlacing of gratitude for his guidance with an unavoidable frustration at the situation. We were always being asked to do more with increasingly less, as if we were conjurors, and it was our duty to rise to the occasion. We had to "make it happen," though it often seemed as if we were expected to be capable of producing something from nothing. Or at least from way too little. And this time, it felt more impossible than ever.

I took a deep breath, trying to steady myself. "Copy that, sir. We'll make it work."

We'll make it work.

How many times did I say those words to myself, feeling resentful but getting on with it regardless? Too many.

As I put down the phone, it was clear the road ahead would be tough. But my team was resilient, and we had a shared purpose. I looked around at my stark surroundings, taking in the environment that was supposed to underpin every mission.

If only we had more resources. If only, if only…

"Master Sergeant Garcia," I called out, determined to face this challenge head on. "We've got some major changes to the mission commander requirements. Let's find a way to make this work."

The words flitted from my mouth despite a lack of certainty that I could even buy into them.

He nodded, without a doubt thinking and feeling just the same, his eyes reflecting a recipe concocted by resolve and exhaustion in equal measures. Together, we dove into planning, discussing options and laying out a strategy.

In a quick meeting with my section chiefs, I laid out the situation. "We're looking at a significant increase in requirements. Five hundred more computers, fifty secure phones."

Their faces registered shock, and I continued, "We're on our own for this. All hands-on deck."

Sergeant Johnson's brows furrowed in thought. "How do we even start, Captain? It does not seem reasonable."

Sergeant Garcia stepped in, outlining our plan, coming up with the unavoidable something from nothing, the proverbial rabbit from the hat. "We'll set up three installation teams, focusing on the tactical ops centers first. One team will work to reconstitute equipment from non-essential areas."

He made it sound so easy. So normal. And that was the sad reality of things; this *was* our normal these days. It was not exactly what we had signed up for, but it was all we were getting nowadays.

There was a moment of silence, a sense of the challenge settling in. Sergeant Hernandez finally spoke up, her voice steady but concerned. "This is a lot, Captain. Are we ready for this?"

I met their gazes, unshakable. "It's a tough mission, but we're a team. We'll make it work. It won't be the first time."

Sergeant Johnson chimed in, "We could leverage mechanics for logistical support, help move the assets."

I nodded, impressed by their commitment. "Great idea. Let's do it."

Sergeant Hernandez added, "We need a clear plan to prioritize equipment installation."

I smiled, grateful for their input. "Exactly. We'll coordinate, ensure we're maximizing our efforts."

As I walked through the busy offices, my team was already in action, working tirelessly to meet the challenge. Master Sergeant Garcia's tired eyes met mine, and despite the hurdles, it could not have been more apparent that we were in this together. Nobody would voice negativity and doubts, not at this time and in this setting. Nobody would say this was not possible, because we knew one thing already—that the purportedly impossible was always achievable. The road ahead was uncertain, but I was determined to lead my team through it, ensuring they knew their well-being remained at the forefront of my mind.

As the evening drew in, uncertainty settled over us. The news of Captain Solomon's recent arrival reached my ears, and I found myself compelled to seek him out. My heart carried a weighty realization, one that had been gnawing at my thoughts for a while. The bond we shared was special, but the demands of our missions were straining it.

I stood at the edge of the vast field of sand and cement, where Captain Solomon was walking, engaged in conversation with a fellow airman. The moment he noticed me, his face lit up in a mix of surprise and worry. He was quick to run over to me.

"Hey, you," he greeted in an affectionate tone. The concern in his eyes didn't pass unnoticed.

I took a deep breath, my heart lurching as I tried to find the right words. "Brian, there's something I need to talk to you about."

His expression shifted as my tone filtered through. "What's on your mind?"

We locked eyes, mine exhibiting both sadness and resolve. "I've been thinking, Brian. About us, about everything. The truth is, our paths are going in different directions, and these missions...they're pulling us apart."

He studied my face, understanding dawning on him. "You mean, our relationship?"

An irrepressible sigh escaped. "Yes, exactly. It's not that I don't care about you or what we have. But the reality is, we both have demanding responsibilities that require our full attention. And if we continue down this path, we'll only end up hurting each other."

His brows furrowed, his gaze searching mine. "Are you saying...you want to end things?"

Tears welled up as I nodded, my voice giving way. "I don't want to, Brian. But I just believe it's the right thing to do. We're meant to support each other, to be there for one another. But if we can't do that, then maybe we're better off as friends."

The words sliced through the distance between us, the feelings they brought almost suffocating us. Brian's heartbreak was real, his silence echoing the depth of his feelings.

"Well. I never imagined it would come to this," he finally managed, his voice sadness itself.

I reached out, gently placing my hand on his. "Brian, please understand. This is tearing me to pieces too. But I can't bear to see us drift apart because of circumstances beyond our control."

He pulled me into a tender hug, holding me as if he never wanted to let go. "I didn't know things would end like this. It doesn't *have to* end like this."

In that moment, in the middle of our bittersweet embrace, our hearts spoke a language of their own, one that went beyond words. It was a painful realization, yet there was also an unspoken understanding between us. Sometimes, love wasn't enough to conquer the challenges life could throw our way. As we held each other, a silent promise of friendship and support lingered, a reminder of the bond we had shared and the memories we would treasure forever.

But I had to be strong, for both of us. With a heavy heart, I gently pulled away from his embrace. "Brian, I...I need to go. Please take care of yourself."

Turning away was the hardest thing I had ever done, each step a painful tug on my heart. As I walked from him, his gaze burned into my back, longing and acceptance interwoven.

I didn't look behind me, couldn't bear to see his heartbreak. The field seemed endless as I walked, steps echoing the heaviness in my heart. The decision had been made, and even though it felt I was leaving a piece of myself behind, I knew it was the right one.

As the distance between us grew, tears were streaming down my face. This was a farewell to a chapter of my life that had brought both joy and pain. But as I walked farther into the evening, I held onto the hope that someday, the timing would be right, and our paths would cross again, bringing a chance for a different kind of love and happiness.

Danger is Close

As the sun dipped below the horizon, the last rays lingered in my office, emanating a subdued radiance in contrast with the challenges looming outside those walls. The hum of activity outside my slightly ajar door served as a constant reminder of the maelstrom of activity that awaited, but for that fleeting moment, I found solace in my workspace cocoon.

As I delved into the sea of reports spread before me, the rhythm of my fingers dancing across the keyboard became a sanctuary, a steady beat anchoring me in the midst of turmoil.

Suddenly, a gentle knock disrupted the harmony of my thoughts. My gaze lifted from the screen, perplexed. The knock had been almost hesitant, as if the one behind it was uncertain about intruding on my solitude. Suspicion mingled with curiosity, compelling me to my feet as I moved toward the source of the sound.

I grasped the doorknob, its cool metal, a stark contrast to the office's warmth. With a slow twist, I tugged the door open, revealing Captain Solomon's presence on the threshold. He stood before me, an enigmatic mixture of brilliance and vulnerability. His eyes, usually so vibrant, seemed to hold a flicker of defeat.

"Captain Solomon, how may I help you?"

His lips curved into a smile, though one that bore a hint of pain that did not reach his eyes. "I have something for you," he responded, extending a hand that held a folded piece of paper, an offering that seemed to carry a far greater importance than its physical presence implied.

I accepted the note, our fingers brushing in the process.

It was a fleeting touch, yet its resonance seemed to linger in the charged air. Our gazes held too for a moment, an unspoken exchange conveying a myriad of messages and feelings before he turned to leave, his retreating steps clattering in the void that remained.

With the door closed once more, I unfolded the note. The inked lines seemed to dance across the page, forming a symphony of sentiments that proclaimed the intricacies of his feelings.

My Dearest Norah,

I am writing to express my unspoken feelings about you and our relationship.

The day our paths crossed is forever etched in my memory.

At that moment, all my worries about computer problems were removed as I caught sight of you.

Your infectious laughter, kindness, and smile stuck out to me.

Since then, every meal shared, and every moment together has made me truly appreciate and treasure the person you are.

Even when I am flying, my thoughts are consumed by the next time I see you.

I understand that our demanding professions create obstacles for our love.

But I believe you're worth it.

Consider it a leap of faith.

However, I respect your decision to end things, whether it's because our paths are diverging or due to something as trivial as the absence of popcorn during our movie night.

Always remember that you have a cherished spot in my heart.

With all my affection,

Brian

Tears welled as I read his letter, each sentence a brushstroke creating a tapestry of longing and affection. My heart swayed in the currents of emotion, caught between the joy of his confession and the fear of an uncertain future. The chair behind me beckoned, and I sank into it, the note resting in my trembling fingers.

Before I could even comprehend everything coursing through my mind, the office door swung open, and there stood Master Sergeant Garcia, his presence grounding, a reminder of the support system that surrounded me. "Captain, we've got a situation." His voice was serious, matching the urgency displayed in his features.

Sergeant Garcia's demeanor spoke volumes. He began to unravel the intricate web of challenges that had sprung forth due to a disruption in the critical communication systems. Another layer of emergency had just woven itself into the already frenetic landscape we were navigating.

Seated in my office, the unfolding crisis pressed down on us. We delved into a meticulous exchange of ideas, each suggestion a chess move in our strategy to regain control over our fractured lines of communication.

The room seemed to hum with the intensity of our team's focus.

"How can we even begin to address this when the heart of the issue lies in Afghanistan?" I mused aloud, a hint of frustration tinging my words.

Sergeant Garcia, always the pragmatic thinker, adjusted his posture as he leaned forward. "Perhaps, Captain, we should approach this from a different angle. Instead of contemplating how we can physically fix the issue from here, let's explore *who* could potentially fix it on the ground."

His perspective opened a new avenue of thought. Together, we began to dissect the problem through this fresh lens. As we deliberated, considering various avenues and potential solutions, the door to our meeting room creaked open, and Airman Bozo entered, a glimmer of determination in his eyes.

"Excuse me, Captain, Sergeant Garcia."

We turned our attention to him, welcoming his presence. "What is it, Airman?" I inquired.

He hesitated for a moment, conviction bolstering his words. "I believe I may have a solution to the communication issues we're facing. If I could get to Hamid Karzai International Airport in Afghanistan, I'm confident I could troubleshoot and restore the critical systems."

Sergeant Garcia and I exchanged a brief glance, surprise and consideration passing between us. "Are you absolutely certain, Airman?" Sergeant Garcia's voice held a hint of skepticism.

Airman Bozo's confidence seemed unshaken. "Yes, sir. I possess the technical expertise required and would only need specific tools to carry out the necessary repairs."

A pause settled over the room as everyone pondered Airman Bozo's proposal.

Sergeant Garcia leaned in closer, his voice a hushed undertone. "Captain, if we entertain this plan, the question remains: how can we ensure Airman Bozo's safe entry into Afghanistan and his access to the airport?"

Our eyes met, minds working in tandem to decipher the complexities of this daring plan. As we contemplated the logistics, my gaze returned to Airman Bozo, and I spoke with a measured tone. "Airman, if we proceed, I'll do my utmost to arrange your transport to Hamid Karzai International Airport. But I must ask one final time: are you absolutely confident that you can resolve the communication issues?"

Airman Bozo's stance stiffened, and he met my gaze head-on. "Yes, Captain!"

A small smile curved my lips as I extended gratitude. "Your courage is admirable, Airman Bozo. May your determination light the path ahead."

Our course of action established, I swiftly left the room, the urgency of the situation propelling me through the night toward the one glimmer of hope that could restore the fractured lines and set our mission back on course.

With a fresh sense of purpose, I headed toward the location where Captain Solomon was sure to be stationed. His confession sat heavily on my mind, urging me forward despite the uncertainty ahead. It might have seemed abrupt and even a touch cruel to confront him like this, without a clear response to his heartfelt words, but I couldn't fathom any other course of action.

There he stood on the verge of stepping out of the building, surprise and intrigue in his expression. We looked at each other. His confusion was evident, yet I could have sworn a flicker of joy danced in his eyes brought on by my unexpected presence. The conflicting emotions in his features tugged at my heart, a pang of both longing and apprehension.

"Hey, is everything all right?" he inquired, his voice showing genuine concern.

I took a deep breath, trying to steady my racing heart.

My steps quickened, making my way toward him, a determined resolve pushing me forward despite the uncertainty in me. His unspoken words hung over me like a storm cloud, and I had to address it, even if the timing felt abrupt and awkward.

As I approached, his presence seemed to illuminate the surroundings in vibrancy. I took a deep breath and began, "I'm sorry for this sudden intrusion, Captain Solomon, but I find myself in a situation where I desperately need your assistance."

His brows furrowed in concern; his curiosity piqued. "Of course, Norah. You know you can count on me. What's going on?"

I met his gaze, staunchly focused as I explained the predicament. "It's about Airman Bozo. The mission-critical communication systems are in disarray, and he believes he has the expertise to fix them. The catch is, we need to get him out to Hamid Karzai International Airport in Afghanistan."

Captain Solomon nodded. "I see. And you need my assistance in arranging transport."

A tense silence enveloped us, our conversation sitting as an uneasy obstacle between us. Captain Solomon's brow furrowed, contemplative, mulling over the situation. The seconds stretched, each passing moment pregnant with unspoken thoughts.

Finally, he broke the silence, his words measured and free of all doubt. "Yeah, all right. I can get Airman Bozo into Afghanistan."

My heart clenched at his willingness, gratitude and concern washing over me. Yet why was I hesitating, my mind racing as I grappled with the reality of his offer? The truth was, all the conflicting anxieties and fears that had been roiling within me were now threatening to spill over, and I found myself needing to voice them all, no matter how vulnerable it made me.

"But do you understand the risks, Brian?" I asked, my voice tinged with a blend of trepidation and urgency. "Flying into such a volatile and uncertain situation..."

He replied calmly, "Look, I know what I'm getting into."

In a moment of anger, I burst. "If I'd known this was what you'd say, I would have never asked you for help."

His gaze held mine, steady. "Why, Norah?"

I shook my head as I stumbled away. He strode closer before gently taking hold of my hand. "Why not, Norah? Why wouldn't you have asked me?"

My breath hitched, caught in crosscurrents. I had to be honest, even if it meant exposing the depths of my soul. "You can't go because...because I care about you too much. More than I should. The mere thought of you in that dangerous scenario...it terrifies me."

The intensity of his gaze was not lost on me, and I was aware that his conviction was unyielding as he leaned in, prompting me to confront my own hesitations. "Norah, look at me. Look at me now. Please."

A sob rose in my throat as I met his stare, the vulnerability of this moment laying me bare, leaving me struggling to find my voice amidst the storm threatening to consume me. He implored again, his words a gentle prod piercing through the barriers I had erected, "What are we doing, Norah? You know how I feel about you. What are you afraid of?"

My voice quivered as I fought to speak my truth, the admission both freeing and agonizing. "I don't want you to fly into Afghanistan, Brian." My love for him was a fragile thread connecting us in the face of uncertainty.

He stepped closer, his touch a grounding force as his hands found their place on my shoulders. He raised my chin with a hand, looking into my eyes as if reading my soul. "Norah, that's not what I'm talking about. And well you know it."

Tears streamed down my cheeks; my vulnerability laid bare. Through the haze, I managed to whisper, "Because I love you."

The shock on his face was undeniable, his features freezing in astonishment and disbelief. The complexity of our situation had deepened with my confession, adding layers of intricacy to the already agonizing decision before us.

Brian's step back was measured, his voice a soft plea amidst the tumultuous sea of our inner thoughts and feelings. "Norah, this is already one of the hardest decisions I've ever had to make. Please don't make it even harder."

My gaze remained locked on him, the profound heartache breaking through the strained silence. His eyes softened, his words a balm to the turmoil raging within me. "You want to know something, Norah? Sometimes, you just have to take a leap of faith. You never know where you might land when you do that."

With those poignant words, he turned away, his footsteps sounding in the distance as he walked off. His final words lingered like a promise, an unspoken commitment that spoke to the depth of our connection. "I'll be ready in four hours," his voice said as it reached me, a lifeline amidst the uncertainty. "Oh, and Norah, don't let me jump alone."

As he faded into the horizon, his words continued to resonate within me, a constant reminder of the choice before me. In that moment, amidst mounting inner thoughts and feelings, I realized that the leap of faith I was considering wasn't just about Airman Bozo or the mission. It was a leap into the unknown, a leap toward a future promising both heartache and the potential for something extraordinary.

The airfield was a hive of activity, the distant hum of engines breathing life into the twilight air as daylight surrendered to an encroaching blackness. Senior Airman Bozo stood before me, a portrait of determination, his gear neatly arranged, ready for his journey. The mission was critical, the disruption in communication systems at Hamid Karzai Airport demanding immediate attention. There was no room for hesitation.

As I stood there, filled with pride and apprehension, a familiar figure approached. Captain Brian Solomon, his presence a beacon of strength amidst the chaos, was walking toward us. The soft glow of the runway lights painted his features in muted hues. He looked as though he had a goal, something definite in mind, but he also showed what I thought was compassion—for me.

"Airman Bozo," I called out, my voice was firm yet displaying genuine concern. "We're counting on you. Take care out there."

Senior Airman Bozo nodded; his gratitude evident as he shook my hand. "Thank you, Captain. I won't let you down."

Tears welled as I realized the magnitude of my decision. Sending our airmen into harm's way, into a land gripped by chaos and uncertainty, was a responsibility I had assumed.

As Brian turned to leave, a knot formed in my throat. I knew what came next. The only way to get Airman Bozo into Afghanistan to address the communication issues was to have Captain Solomon pilot the aircraft to take him there. My heart ached at the thought, for I had come to care deeply for Brian, and the idea of him flying into danger tore at my insides.

The C-17 transport aircraft loomed before us, a massive silhouette against the dimming sky. I watched as Senior Airman Bozo boarded, disappearing into the cavernous interior of the plane. Captain Solomon's voice interrupted my thoughts, his words a soothing balm.

"Navigating uncertainty is part of our duty, Norah," he said softly, his gaze steady as it met mine. "Sometimes, we must step into the unknown to make a difference."

His statement offered a depth of meaning that resonated, a reminder of the sacrifices we all made, the risks we undertook to fulfill our missions. But in his eyes, there was far more—a reflection of the bittersweet truth lying between us. We had formed a connection, a bond that defied the chaos around us.

Before I could find the words to respond, Brian handed me a small slip of paper. I unfolded it, my eyes scanning the words. "Peace, I leave with you; my peace I give you. Do not let your hearts be troubled, and do not be afraid."

Tears welled again as I looked up at him, my voice barely above a whisper. "Brian, I..."

He silenced me with a gentle touch to my shoulder, his eyes conveying an understanding that ran deeper than words. "Norah, this is the path we've chosen. We'll find our way through it, together. Yes?"

He waited for my nod, and I delivered it, unable to speak anymore.

As the C-17 taxied down the runway, its engines roaring to life, I watched through tear-blurred vision. The emotional burden on me was undeniable, but so was the determination as it burned inside me. Brian's sacrifice, our shared commitment—it was a testament to the strength that resided within each of us.

The aircraft lifted off, disappearing into the night sky, and I took a deep breath, steeling myself for the challenges ahead. Swallowing my emotions, I turned to face the chaos around, knowing that even amidst uncertainty, a steadfast resolve bound us all.

The departure of both Brian and Airman Bozo had left me anxious and rattled, my office now a sanctuary of irrepressible sentiments. Helplessness gnawed at me, an unfamiliar sensation for someone accustomed to being in control. We hovered over the desk, restless and fidgety, as if seeking to physically grapple with the reality of a non-tangible situation.

With a deep exhalation, I realized that I needed to seek solace in the one place that had always provided comfort—family. Pulling out my phone, I dialed my grandfather's number.

Longing coursed through me.

"Hello?" His voice, warm and familiar, acted as a soothing balm.

"Hi, Grandpa," I greeted, my voice trembling. "How are you holding up?"

He chuckled softly, a sound that carried a world of affection. "Oh, you know, the usual aches and pains of old age. But enough about me, how are you, my dear?"

My voice quivered. "I don't know, Grandpa. It's all so overwhelming."

He would have sensed the urgency in my tone. "Tell me about it, sweetheart. What's on your mind?"

I closed my eyes, drawing strength from his presence even through the phone. "There's someone, Grandpa. Someone important to me. But the circumstances, the challenges...I'm not sure if it's even possible."

He listened patiently, his support a lifeline in this moment of vulnerability. "Norah, my dear, life is fleeting. Don't let fear or uncertainty hold you back from pursuing what you want."

The tears still cascaded free. "But, Grandpa, what if it's too complicated?"

A thoughtful pause followed, his wisdom intermingling with the silence. "Ah, my dear, life is full of complexities. But sometimes, taking that leap of faith is the only way to find clarity."

"Thank you, Grandpa. Your guidance means the world to me."

Amidst my tearful gratitude, his voice remained a steady presence. "Norah, you've always had a strength within you. Remember that. Life's journey is like a river with its twists and turns. Keep moving forward, no matter the challenges, Norah. That's what life is about."

A smile tugged at my lips, his mention of my grandmother evoking cherished memories. But there was more he wanted to share, a revelation bridging our generations.

"Norah, let me share a secret. Back in my youth, I was much like you are now—uncertain, hesitant. It took me years to gather the courage to express my feelings to your grandmother."

His vulnerability struck a chord within me, deepening our connection in ways I hadn't fully realized. "Ha! Really? And look where it led you, Grandpa."

His voice mellowed, tender affection evident in every word. "Exactly. You have that same courage within you, my dear. Embrace it."

A lump formed in my throat. "Thank you, Grandpa."

"Lillian is always watching over you, Norah. Remember that."

With his reassurance to lean on, I ended the call, my spirits lifted. Taking a deep breath, I wiped away my tears, finding a renewed sense of purpose. Life's challenges *were* formidable, but with the wisdom of generations behind me, facing them head on was viable.

As the sun began its pinked descent, I stood among the excited chatter of my team, waiting with bated breath. Senior Airman Bozo had been inside that plane, tasked with a mission that could change the course of our efforts. Anxiety and hope were mingling.

Restlessness gnawed at my insides as I paced back and forth in the communication center, my gaze fixated on the large monitors displaying data streams and incoming messages. The room was a hive of activity, team members hunched over their stations, their fingers dancing across keyboards as they worked tirelessly to establish a connection. My heart raced, and I couldn't help but voice the question, "Any word from Captain Solomon? How's the mission progressing?"

A technician looked up from his screen, his expression focused yet tinged with empathy. "We're still working on it, Captain. So far, there hasn't been any response."

I clenched my jaw. "Keep trying. We need to know if they're okay."

Throughout the room, heads nodded in agreement, fingers redoubling their efforts too. The tension was in everyone's minds, and in mine more so. Every beep of an incoming message made my heart skip a beat, only to sink when it wasn't the news we had been awaiting.

Minutes turned into an eternity, each passing second adding to the mounting tension. And then, like a beacon of light, a series of cheers erupted from the control center. Relief surged, a collective sigh of triumph as the news spread—Senior Airman Bozo had done it. He had resolved the communication issues, bringing a triumphant end to our forty-eight-hour sprint.

Amid the jubilation, I could hardly contain my emotions. I approached a group of technicians, my voice trembling slightly. "He's on his way back, I take it?"

A young woman turned to me, a grin lighting up her face. "Yes, Captain. He's on his way. ETA is approximately four hours."

My shoulders grew lighter, pride and gratitude flooding my heart. "Thank you," I whispered.

Pride swelled in my chest as I watched my team embrace, hearing laughter, seeing the many congratulatory pats on the back. The sense of camaraderie was palpable, a testament to the teamwork that had carried us through this ordeal. I couldn't help but smile, my heart brimming for each member who had poured their heart and soul into this endeavor.

Amid the jubilation, I kept my eyes fixed on the horizon, anticipation building with each passing moment. And then, as if on cue, the distinct hum of engines thrummed, and the plane touched down, a symbol of triumph and resilience. I watched as the aircraft taxied toward us.

As the cargo door opened, Senior Airman Bozo emerged, exhaustion on his face but a triumphant gleam in his eyes. I hurried forward, a tray of warm food in hand.

"You did it," was all I said, and it was more than enough.

He grinned tiredly, accepting the food. "We did it, thanks to the team's hard work."

Master Sergeant Garcia and the team gathered around him, ready to guide him back to lodging and ensure he got the well-deserved rest he needed. As the group gradually dispersed, my heart raced in anticipation, nervous excitement coursing through me.

And then, with the setting sun almost gone, he appeared.

Brian, my heart's desire. He moved with purpose, his gaze locked onto mine, and before I knew it, he was right in front of me. Without a word, he scooped me up into his arms, the world around us fading into a blur as he pressed his lips to mine in a kiss that held all the longing, all the unspoken words.

When we finally pulled apart, our breaths intermingling, he held me close, his eyes sparkling. "Norah," he began, his voice filled with a tenderness that sent shivers down my spine.

A smile formed on my face, unable to contain myself in his presence. "You know," I interjected softly. "There's a story about them that I think you'd appreciate."

His gaze remained fixed on mine; curiosity evident in the furrow of his brow. "I'm all ears."

I took a moment to compose myself, my heart fluttering like a fragile bird in my chest.

"My grandmother always told me about the day my grandfather knocked on her door unexpectedly. She wasn't prepared for it at all, and he looked into her eyes and said, 'I've been through living hell, and my worst regret would have been if I'd never had the chance to tell you how I feel about you.'"

Brian's smile widened, a knowing twinkle in his eyes. His fingers gently brushed a strand of hair from my face. "Your grandparents were wise souls."

I chuckled. "They were indeed. And you know, their story reminds me that sometimes, life's greatest regrets come from not taking a chance on love."

He leaned in, his voice a gentle caress between us. "Norah, you've shown me the importance of embracing the present and seizing opportunities. Life's unpredictable, and I've come to realize that waiting for the 'right' moment can lead to regrets. So, I'm wondering, would you consider taking a chance with me?"

As his words floated between us, my heart flipped. His question was profound, and a rush of emotions came over me. A soft smile formed, and I met his gaze with an affectionate glint in my gaze. "Brian," I murmured. "I think it's time we embrace the journey together."

And in that fleeting moment, beneath the canvas of another sunset that was slipping away, our tacit understanding spoke volumes. With a shared smile, we embarked on this new chapter, a leap of faith holding the promise of a beautiful future intertwined with love and endless possibilities.

As weeks turned into months, I came to realize the deeper meaning behind the challenges life had thrown my way. My first month of deployment had been made up of craziness, each obstacle a reminder of the unpredictability of life. My grandfather's words had stayed in my mind, his courage to take a chance for love serving as a beacon of inspiration.

And so, as the days unfolded, Brian and I navigated the uncertainties together, our love serving as a guiding light. We faced each challenge as it came along, our connection growing stronger with each passing moment.

One day, as I entered my office, I noticed something different—a message scrawled across the whiteboard in bold letters. "The Military Mustang." My heart swelled. My team, my commander, had left this as a testament to our journey, a reminder of the resilience and unity that had carried us through.

In that simple yet profound message, I found closure, a sense of fulfillment stirring deep within me. Love, like life, was a journey of unexpected twists and turns. And as I looked ahead, hand in hand with Brian, I knew that the path we had chosen was one worth traveling, a leap of faith that had led us to places we had never imagined.

Acknowledgements

My heart overflows with gratitude to those who have shaped my path and inspired me to strive for greatness. To each one of you, I express my heartfelt thanks:

Above all, I am indebted to God for His unmerited favor, unwavering grace, and divine blessings, which have been a constant source of inspiration and comfort on this journey of self-discovery.

To Mom, Dad, and my dear sister, thank you for your unyielding love and support, which have been a life-giving force, especially during my darkest hours. You have been my rock, my refuge, and my shining light.

I also want to thank my little girl, Georgia, whose innocent joy and boundless energy continue to inspire me to cherish life's simple pleasures and embrace all its beauty, no matter the challenges that come my way.

To my grandparents, I am forever grateful for your unwavering faith in me, limitless wisdom, and endless love that have built the foundation of my life.

To the one who opened my eyes to a new world, this is for you. Your faith in God has inspired me, your gentle kindness has shown me grace, and your loving nature has deeply impacted me.

A special thanks to Chief Master Sergeant Christopher Jones for his insightful advice and unwavering support in challenging me to discover and embrace my "why" for commissioning. It's because of you that I have grown into a better officer and a better person.

My heartfelt gratitude to Brigadier General Chad Raduege, Colonel James Riley, and Lieutenant Colonel Nicholas DeAngelis for endorsing my commissioning package, paving the way for me to serve alongside some of the most outstanding Airmen.

I cannot forget to thank the selfless men and women who serve our country's armed forces with honor and commitment, making the impossible possible every day. Your bravery, sacrifice, and dedication have earned my utmost respect and admiration.

About the Author

Brandon Seyl, born and raised in Warner Robins, Georgia, enlisted in the United States Air Force when he was nineteen, embarking on a remarkable military career. He excelled during Basic Military Training, graduating as an Honor Graduate.

Brandon then went on to serve in Air Force Special Operations as well as with the White House Communications Agency, supporting both Presidents Obama and Trump. Upon being selected to attend Officer Training School, Brandon graduated with distinction, earning the title of Distinguished Graduate in 2019. Today, he remains an active member of the Air Force and has deployed on five missions supporting Operation ENDURING FREEDOM, Operation SPARTAN SHIELD, and Operation ALLIES REFUGE.

Beyond his impressive military service, Brandon finds great fulfillment in his hobbies. He is an enthusiastic advocate for sea turtle conservation efforts and animal welfare causes more broadly. Brandon is passionate about preserving endangered species and doing his part to protect the planet. He also loves to travel and has visited numerous countries and cultures, broadening his perspective and enriching his experiences.

Brandon's most profound joy comes from spending quality time with his daughter, Georgia. Despite his demanding schedule, he treasures every moment they share to build a lasting, meaningful relationship with her.

Even with his busy schedule and personal interests, Brandon remains fully committed to his fellow Airmen, advocating for their well-being and guiding them in their military careers to find meaning and purpose. He is driven to help others overcome challenges and achieve their goals, as evidenced in his book, "The Military Mustang." Brandon shares his journey to inspire and encourage others. His story serves as a testament to perseverance and determination, with the hope of inspiring others to overcome adversity and find their paths to fulfillment.